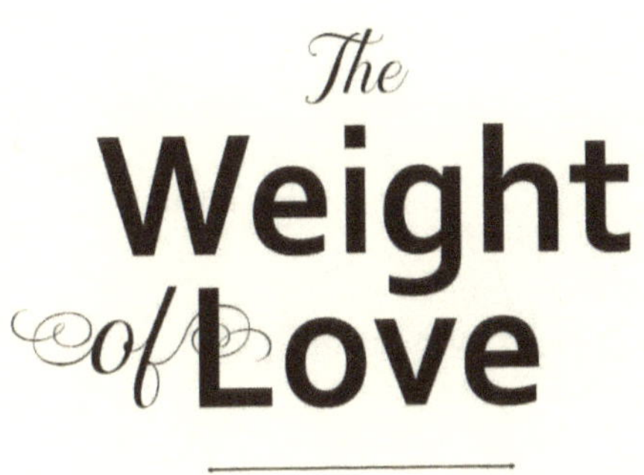

The Weight *of* Love

A Novel

SUNNA BOHLEN

Library of Congress Cataloging-in-Publication Data
Bohlen, Sunna, 1950 –
The weight of love

ISBN: 978-1-7337557-0-2 (print)
        978-1-7337557-1-9 (ePub)
        978-1-7337557-2-6 (Kindle)

Cover design by S. M. Savoy
Cover image: Painting by Sunna Bohlen, *When You Call
          Me Yellow, I Feel Blue*, copyright © 2003
Photo credit: Martin Fritz

Foreword

Sunna Bohlen is a remarkable woman.

I should know — we have been friends for more than 40 years. Her creative energy has always impressed me. Over her long career, Sunna has distinguished herself in the visual arts and in poetry, but she also excels in the culinary arts. I have been fortunate to share many meals with her.

Sunna's painting and poetry is infused with a strong energetic force, reflecting serenity and pathos, as does her life. She is a courageous adventurer, a fearless spirit, using occasional problems as stepping-stones along the path to her destination. She lives and loves passionately. But what I most admire in Sunna is her resilience, her ability to recover from life's unfortunate turmoil.

Now this unique survivor has written a novel, sharing the motivations and inspirations for her art, her resilience, and her life. Her book will touch your life, and you will never be the same.

Roger Guillemin is a French-born, American neuroscientist.
He was awarded the Nobel Prize in Medicine in 1977.

Author's Note

From an early age, I have felt a great compulsion to investigate the human condition, life's balancing act of survival and transcendence. Language and philosophy were the first tools I used to extract and abstract the meaning of my experiences and understand the feelings and thoughts behind them.

Through my art, I have tried to translate more than the aesthetic quality of my work, insisting on the connection between my emotions and the natural world by combining various mental and physical environments.

Through creative struggle, these worlds come together beyond the limits of duality. In my negotiations with reality, I sometimes find that I understand myself and the world more clearly when I gaze beyond my physical boundaries and pursue a vision of immaterial energies, which may help decode our humanity and our existence in the world.

Today, I am committed to conveying these feelings through painting, writing, and cooking. For me, these are acts of emotional survival, providing a means to reconcile the intimate inexplicability of the human psyche. With this creative synthesis, my work becomes a ritual gesture of conscious healing.

As many artists do, I base my creative work on things that have happened to me, things I have seen, and my interpretations of emotions and events. I am grateful to all of my family, friends, and partners for the support they've offered me at different times, and for the growth they've inspired me to achieve. This story should in no way be interpreted as an attempt to portray the reality of my relationships. I have tried to honor my experiences and stay true to my feelings, but this book is a work of fiction. I hope it will inspire others to resilience.

Acknowledgements

Very special recognition must be given to my life-long friends, Dr. Roger and Madame Lucianne Guillemin. Because of your encouragement, I developed a passion for life and was privileged to become part of your amazing family. You have given me many opportunities to achieve otherwise unachievable dreams, and I am forever grateful to you both.

The following people have provided valuable insights and guidance. I truly appreciate the confidence each of you have shown in my art, poetry, cooking, and friendship. You have my deepest gratitude.

Prof. Dr. Elizabeth Blackburn
Dr. Friedrich & Dr. Anna von Bohlen
Dr. Gr. Bernhard Broermann
Herr Nikolai Burkart
Dr. Peter Farrell
Madame Francoise Gilot
Dr. Giza & Mrs. Elizabeth von Habsburg
Dr. Nabil & Dr. Gayda Hana
Mr. Sam & Mrs. Reena Horowitz
Dr. Suzann Kirchner Brouns
Mrs. Carol Lazier
Madame Reinette & Mr. Marvin Levin
Dr. Stewart & Mrs. Lisa Lipton

Herr Gr. Friedrich von Löbbecke
Dr. Merle Naponic
Monsieur Hélie de Noailles
Dr. David & Mrs. Mary Beth Oblon
Prof. Dr. Frederik Paulsen
Dr. Richard della Penna
Dr. Rudolf & Frau Isabelle Rüedi
Herr Gerhard Schöningh
Dr. Eli & Dr. Liz Shefter
Mr. Gurjit & Mrs. Neeru Singh
Dr. Thomas Widman
Mrs. Armi & Mr. Al Williams
Mrs. Judy & Mr. Jack White

To my editor, Alissa Jones Nelson, I couldn't have done it without you!

This book is dedicated to my children, Daniel and Thomas; to my grandchildren, Justin and Alex; and to my daughter-in-law Michiru, with gratitude for their unconditional love. There are no words to express how I feel, and I am eternally grateful to each of you for loving me as a mother, grandmother, and mother-in-law.

Contents

Chapter 1:
Sprout

Diminutia,
every life is a rarity
producing
a unique episode
by virtue of growth.

A sprout
has no concern,
no vision,
but is wise enough to see
a cruel reality.

Vulnerable
as it seems,
a hopeful dream
is a sign of life.
Sprout shoots up, arouses awe.

For me, Berlin has always been a place of healing. A place to overcome divisions, break down walls. Here, far from the spirits that trouble the sea, I paint my life onto canvas and hang it on the walls of my apartment. At night, my paintings reflect against the window glass as if they're floating in the air outside. They adorn the sandstone walls of the old church across the square. Berlin is the perfect spiritual haven for anyone who doesn't believe in spirits.

I paint my internal landscape. I paint raw emotion,

but somehow the finished canvases are calming. I don't paint every day. It all depends on intensity. I gather my experience, my feeling, my need, until it all erupts without warning. Then I sit in my studio for hours, even days, sometimes without food, without speaking. It's a shamanic experience. My art is my mother's shadow.

The poetry comes differently. I lift it out of my intellectual life. It rises from events, relationships, nodes I can pinpoint. It is the result of long spools of thought, my own philosophical thread. My principle of resilience. An attitude to life I have reformulated and rebuilt over and over again. The words on the page anchor me, even as the paintings float free in the night.

I have always loved to be deep within myself, discovering. Early on, I learned to like my own company best. But it has taken a lifetime to learn to cultivate solitude. To nurture it and let its roots grow deep, so that it endures the desiccation of drought and the force of flood. In the end, everything feels better when I'm alone. As I am now. Again, or at last. Perhaps not for long.

I've spent my life giving myself away. In the process, I've learned how to nurture myself as a foundation for loving others. The lessons of love have been painful, and beautiful. The weight of it all grounds me even as new love buoys me up.

In Berlin, I'm finally free of the anxiety the ocean has always called up in me. I feel safe. The sea is the most powerful force in nature. For me it has been a wellspring of trauma and beauty both. Like every experience in life. Someday, I'll return to the sea.

I was born the morning the Korean War began. Or the war was born the morning I began. There are at least two ways to see everything.

In wartime, you accept without questioning. It's the only way to survive. From a very early age, I felt suffocated by secrets. There were no explanations, only stories.

My father was the richest man in our town, but I grew up believing I was the daughter of a ghost. From the time I was just a week old, I lived under my father's tile roof. Five tin roofs separated me from the packed earth floor where my mother slept. As a young child, I would pass her in the street as if she were a stranger. Even though we were both well aware that her womb had been my first home, I was forbidden to speak to her. Feeling the throb of her blood in my veins, I dreaded becoming her.

In my first real memory of her, she is a wandering spirit, her white robes and long black hair floating in the salt wind off the sea. She passes our house on silent feet, a bowl of shadowed fruit balanced on the crown of her head, silhouetted against the round face of the full moon. I sit on the porch, huddled against the chimney for warmth, afraid to go inside, where my father's anger submerges the rooms and sucks the air from my lungs. I watch as she drifts down to the sand, and when she is just

a black emptiness against the sudden shimmer of breaking waves, I follow. I hear her murmur as the waves pull
back. She seems to be speaking to someone, her palms
pressed together in prayer, words escaping her chapped
lips, flung away on the wind. I creep closer, holding
my breath, waiting for the moon to open its suggestive
mouth and answer. But her entreaties meet with silence
from above, while the chaos of the waves swirls around
her knees and soaks her thin tunic. She sinks into the wet
sand, keening, and I stand off to the side, chilled, feeling
nothing at all.

As I grew older, my mother terrified me in all her absur-
dity. Where others in our windswept town saw a liturgy,
an appeal to the ancestors who inhabited the salty air all
around us, I saw only celestial psychosis.

Sunyi, our housekeeper, had come with my father
when he left my grandfather's household to start his own
family. One night, drifting high on too much rice wine
from her secret stash, she told me my first story.

"Your parents were teenage lovers. You should have
seen your mother then. A bamboo stick, thin and hollow, with a wild spirit trapped inside. Your father was
bewitched. Just before his twenty-first birthday, he asked
your grandfather to arrange the marriage. But your grandfather abhorred her restless spirit. A girl like that will
never breed stability. There's too much of the sea in her.
I stood outside the door while your father waited for his
father's answer. Your grandfather stared at his bent head
and folded hands for the time it takes to boil tea. He left

the room without a word. The next day, we were ordered to give your father nothing but plain rice to eat. To teach his son the simple realities of life, he said. But I heard your father say that each grain reminded him of your mother, dressed all in white, feeding the whole town."

My mother went around town proclaiming her sightings of gods and the messages they gave her. Even then, when she was just a girl, the townspeople looked to her for guidance. She helped them navigate the spirit world, and in return they called her shaman. She made up for her wild behavior with predictions sharp as arrows, hitting her targets with precision and truth. She could tell a mother when her daughter would marry. A son whether his father would recover from cancer. She could see fate, whether suffering or reward, and the townspeople trusted her to tell the truth without blinking. The world was small then, and people needed something immediate to believe in. They gave her their last pennies in exchange for the authentic vision of themselves they saw in her steady gaze. But my grandfather saw something different. He looked into her wide, bright eyes and saw illness and disgrace.

"Your father was always as stubborn and brutal as he is now. He ate almost nothing for weeks. Many thick foggy mornings, when I went to fetch water, I saw him sneaking back into the house through the window of his room. But his father's judgment poisoned them, as happens to so many. One morning, when the sun had just painted a bloody line on the wall over the bed, he finally saw in her sleeping face everything his father had seen: an affliction where there had been a gift, frenzy mistaken for beauty. And it's like that for all of us. Clouds scuttle across the night sky and it seems the stars themselves are moving. But once you see it's the clouds flying and the stars are fixed, you can't ever convince the stars to move again."

As my mother cleaved to her visions, wound tighter in the shrouds of the spirits, my father began to unravel. He needed a wife who would nourish him. In his mind, the sea, the pine trees, and the moon were all competitors for her love. So he returned to my grandfather's house and humbly declared his willingness to marry whomever his father chose for him. He rushed down the beaten path of an arranged marriage.

I have no idea whether my father and stepmother were ever happy. By the time I was old enough to weigh their love, whatever joy may once have lit their life together had been battered and dragged under by the waves of fate. Their first child, a girl, brought shame on the family in a world where only boys were valued. Only boys were worthy of education or inheritance. Only boys carried on the family name. A year later, another little girl was born. She lived a few fragile days, and died of a mysterious illness. No one mourned for her. She was not what was desired.

My grandfather blamed my stepmother. Not for his granddaughter's death, which didn't concern him, but for her failure to produce a son. He was a patient man. He waited ten years, but the boy he longed for never came. Finally, as was common in such cases in those days, he arranged a surrogate for my father. A single girl in the village, young and vital, who would provide the desired heir. For reasons of his own, he chose the village shaman.

I've often wondered what my father felt as my mother's expanding belly rounded out her white tunic like a waxing moon. Hope, perhaps. The sense of having come full circle. If fate had given him a son, he might have lived a different life. He might have been a different man.

But fate gave my father another girl, born into the world through the tunnel of a fierce, inquisitive spirit. A girl with the shaman's eyes. Resentment reached in and squeezed my father's heart, and it never let him go.

Shortly before I was born, when war loomed like a tanker on the horizon, my father took several precautions to ensure a safe escape to Japan in case the worst should happen. He hired laborers to cut a steep staircase into the cliffs behind the house, hired fishermen to build a dock, and anchored a large boat in the cove. As my mother's birth screams ended and my first cry filled the air, he watched with satisfaction as his builders bolted a thick metal door over a concrete bunker next to his house. From the time I came under his roof until the war ended, I slept there every night. Sunyi carried me down into the earth as the light faded from the sky. My infant dreams were weighted down by the heavy drone of American bombers. The bunker was heated by a single stove, and we slept around it like a cold spiral galaxy clustered around the sun. The warmest places next to the stove went to my father and stepmother. My older sister curled up nearby.

The servants slept at a respectful distance, swaddled in rough wool blankets.

My stepmother's distaste for me was never a secret. It could have been different. She had lost one of her own daughters, and here was another baby to fill her empty arms. But the wound in her heart had scabbed over, and she was not willing to tear it open for me. When I arrived at the house, there was no one to nurse me. Sunyi gave me rice milk and honey to drink and expected me to die within a few weeks. Another lost girl pressed into the earth under a tombstone of expectation and disappointment. On my first night down in the bunker, unwilling to coddle me herself, my stepmother sent me to sleep with the maids, far from the warmth of the stove.

In the morning, wakened by my cries, Sunyi was shocked to find my face frozen where my cheek had rested on the cold tile floor. She brought me to the stove, chaffed my face with her coarse blanket, and heated rice milk to give me. But my lips remained frozen, unable to suck from the bottle. Even when I screamed with the pain, my left eye stayed open, demanding an explanation from the world.

Reluctantly, my father sent for the town herbalist. As a remedy, the healer boiled medicinal herbs and seared them into my skin to bring it back to life. He pricked my cheeks with needles to block the nerve paths and prevent the damage from spreading. The feeling returned to my face, but the treatment left me with permanent nerve damage.

As long as I can remember, I've had a constant pain

behind my left ear. I don't hear well, smiling is nearly impossible, and my left eyelid doesn't close all the way, leaving me hypersensitive to air and light. On that day, I became not merely a burden, an unwanted girl, the daughter of a crazy woman. I was damaged goods.

But I survived. I grew. My sister and I bore the brunt of my father's disappointment. Miha was ten years old when I was born. Already she carried the scars of abuse, on her skin and in her heart. Whatever affection my stepmother may have felt for her daughter was no match for the shame my grandfather heaped over her. Miha needed me as much as I needed her. From the time I could walk, it was clear that she would be the only one to guide me.

I never saw my father cry. I imagine many children can say the same. But I never saw him laugh, either. The only familiar emotion was anger. In our house, I had no reflection. All the mirrors had been destroyed in fits of rage, shattered by flying furniture. The shards of glass ringing across the floor seemed to satisfy my father even as they prodded the rest of us to imagine what more he might be capable of. After one of his rages, when he'd scattered shredded furniture through the house like matchsticks, he would go to the attic with several packs of cigarettes and a chamber pot and wouldn't come down for days. The smell of cigarette smoke leaking down through the floorboards was a comfort, an assurance that we were safe for the time being. After days without sustenance, he would emerge, serene, and Sunyi would go up to empty the chamber pot and sweep up the cigarette butts.

Outside of our house, he was a different man. The neighbors knew him to be generous and dignified. He always gave to anyone in need, even strangers. He never touched a drop of alcohol. He abhorred any public loss of control. Standing at the window after dinner, he would watch the fishermen, drunk after a day on the shivering sea, fighting and rolling in the dusty street. "Dogs," he'd spit at the glass.

In those days, we lived at the edge of the world. Beyond our windows, nothing but waves upon waves separated us from Japan. Two roads converged at our front door, awash in sunshine, sea breezes, and refugees from the North. They slept by the side of the road, wrapped in blankets, waiting for their chance. The boats in the harbor ferried fish, passengers, and black market goods all bundled together in rotting holds. There was no lock on our door, and my father made a point of inviting anyone who was hungry to eat with us. As the largest landowner in town, his storerooms were full of food, and his maids fed the laborers, the farmers, and any hungry refugees who happened to be crowded onto our porch. Many of these women spent the night in my father's room, exchanging what they could for his generosity to them and their children. They drifted through our house like ghosts, haunting the blank spaces between my father's public persona and his private rage. Years later, as each new year broke over the old one, I would marvel at the crates of crisp apples, baskets of persimmons, and boxes of exotic pastries that arrived at our door to thank my father for his time-worn hospitality.

I was four years old and the listless refugees were long gone when I saw my first American soldier. All my life, they had colonized our imaginations and fleshed the specters of our dreams: stories of tall broad men with eyes like the sea and hair like standing wheat. One afternoon Sunyi came rushing into my room, flung all the linen from my futon cabinet onto the floor, and used her teeth and fingernails to tear my oldest sheet into long strips. I couldn't catch my breath in time to ask what she was doing. The wailing from our neighbor's house was my first clue. The woman had been shot as she was gathering mushrooms in the forest. As Sunyi wound the makeshift bandages tight around her shoulder and one of the other maids ran to fetch the healer, the women wailed out a strange word over and over again, like a mantra: "Yanqui! Yanqui!" I rained questions down on Sunyi, but she just pressed her lips together and wiped the peppery blood from her hands.

The next day, the tallest man I had ever seen arrived at the edge of town. The neighbor children clustered on the pine-dark hill overlooking the intersection in front of my father's house. As the golden-haired giant drew nearer, I could see the sun glinting off a long black metal tube strapped across his chest.

"Yanqui! Yanqui!" shrieked the children on the ridge. Panic stricken, I lunged up from the porch and tore into the house, tripping over a rug and struggling back to my feet as the screams pushed louder through the walls. I rushed to my room and, as I'd seen Sunyi do, I tore the sheets and blankets from the futon cabinet and hid myself inside. I stayed there, listening to the sound of my own breath, while Korean whispers filtered through the dusty air and the sound of foreign words, bright and clear as temple bells, pierced my hiding place like bullets. My sister found me there. She coaxed me out, and together we crept on bare, silent feet to the porch. There, next to my father and Mr. Kim, one of the teachers at the school, the Yanqui sat cross-legged and slouching. His gun lay next to him on the ground. I gasped so loud the whole group turned to us, and the soldier grinned with all his teeth.

Mr. Kim nodded at the Yanqui's words and stumbled through his own replies. My father waved an imperious hand to shush Sunyi and a few of the other women who were hissing quiet questions in Korean. The soldier reached into his backpack and produced a bag of something that clacked like the seashell anklet my mother wore when she danced through town. I drew back as he held it out to me. He looked into my eyes and said something, shaking the bag, but I clasped my hands behind my back and shook my head. My father squinted and made a sound low in his throat, and my knees started to quake. Mr. Kim let out something between a laugh and a sigh and reached for the bag, ripping off a corner and pouring the contents into his palm. Little round jewels emerged in bright red, green, and yellow, along with others the color of mud. The soldier reached for Mr. Kim's hand and popped one of these gems into his mouth, crunching away behind his big white teeth. Mr. Kim took one himself, smiling and nodding at the blond giant. My sister, braver than I was, took an emerald pebble from her teacher's palm and popped it into her mouth. Then Mr. Kim held his hand out to me. My father prodded me with one long finger. The candy tasted like sugar and butter and sand, and it crunched like raw peas. I wrinkled my nose, and the ocean-eyed soldier laughed.

Mr. Kim explained to us later that the man was the leader of the Yanqui soldiers, that one of his men had been hunting in the forest above the town and had mistaken our neighbor for a deer. The American had explained this mistake as though it was obvious, since the differences between us were so great. They seemed to think we looked like forest fauna. The soldier brought the M&Ms as a peace offering. To me, they looked like another kind of weapon. Bullets dressed in beautiful colors.

From then on, soldiers appeared frequently in our small town. News of their presence always carried on the wind in their ringing words and their machine-gun laughter. The other children learned to anticipate the candy they always received from their big rough hands, hands like those of the farmers on my father's land. Even my sister learned to like their sugary treats. But I rushed to hide whenever I heard them. It was as if I could already see my future coming down the street after them, the barrel of its gun snaking between their broad shoulders, aimed squarely at my heart.

A boy born into a family like mine would have had plenty of leisure time. Girls were another matter. My stepmother expected my sister and I to help in the kitchen alongside the servants. We may have been wealthy, but with war's long tail snaking through the countryside, there was still no electricity and no running water. Every convenience was always approaching, never arriving. In the foggy seaside dawn, I went with the maids to fetch water at the stream. The men in town chopped firewood to feed our ravenous stove. Everyone had to work. And I made lots of mistakes. Sunyi would throw up her hands and swat me on the crown of my head. She called me Thunder – quick but chaotic, sometimes destructive. But I learned quickly. By the time I was six, I could gut and scale a fish faster than anybody else in my father's kitchen. I loved the buzz of garlic in my nose, the sting of hot chili on my hands. I developed a reputation for swift hands and the ability to accomplish many things at once. I earned a new nickname, one my sister gifted me – Octopus. One head, many talents.

I was proud of my skill. Even so, there were plenty of reasons to hate myself. All I had to do was believe my stepmother when she told me I was unwanted. All I had to do was stand before my father when he summoned me, listen to him describe all the ways I was just like my worthless mother. All the features he found repulsive because they were hers. All I had to do was sit still and watch as the other children moved past my father's house in packs, staring, pointing and laughing behind their hands.

My first day of school clarified any doubts I might have had about why the other children in town hated me. Learning the contours of their poverty made it easy to hate myself too. Slung over my shoulder, I carried a beautiful embossed leather bag, a gorgeous present my uncle brought back from one of his trips to Japan. My classmates made do with dirty cloth sacks. I wore the wristwatch he gave me, a narrow rectangular face on a burgundy band cinched around my thin wrist. None of the other children could dream of owning such a thing. They starved during the school day and froze all through the winter. I saw myself as they saw me, eating my three meals a day and bundling into my thick padded coat when the first freezing needles of rain darted off the ocean. When they pulled my hair and pushed me down, when they ripped the bag from my shoulder and stomped my watch into the dirt, some tiny stone in my chest opened its mouth and told me they were right. Nevertheless, I made it a point never to let them see me cry. To them, my nickname was Solitary Stone.

So I had entered the world as thunder, and I had made myself into the octopus who swallowed a stone. I felt it in my core, solid, secret. I couldn't swallow it down, and I couldn't force it up. Every time my father slapped me, every time my stepmother spit her knife-bladed words, every time another child stared across the schoolyard with hungry eyes, that hard lump grew a little, like molten lava dropping into the sea. I felt the hiss and sting of it. Eventually, I thought, it would crowd out everything else and I'd be an island all on my own.

But I also had another option. I could cultivate the octopus. Roll the stone over. Use my talents to chip away at it. That was when I learned that soft salted noodles and flakey boiled mackerel were more substantial and enduring than the slate cliffs leading down to the sea.

There was always someone looking after me, although it was never my parents. Thanks to Miha and Sunyi, my black-lacquered stacking lunchbox was always full of good things. Spicy dried fish and charcoal-grilled vegetables. Salted eel and sharp pickled sardines. Seaweed that tasted of deep water. Kimchi that burned my lips. One day it occurred to me like one of Sunyi's knocks on the head that I could always get more, like waves advancing and retreating on the shore. If I skipped lunch, I could just eat when I got back to my father's kitchen after school.

So I started giving my lunches away. First to my sometime friend, a smart girl named Jangmi who learned that if she sat next to me and braved the other children's stares, she could eat my food while I went hungry. But there were always more empty mouths, and if I didn't fill them with food, they'd pour out abuse instead. Like little stone pitchers filled with their parents' bitterness and their own gnawing want. I asked Sunyi for more food, bigger lunches, but my little lunchbox would only hold so much, and my stepmother worried about me getting fat, which would make it harder to marry me off. But there was always food in the storeroom. And I knew how to prepare it.

One day after school, I invited several of the other children home with me. Most of them had only ever seen my father's house from the outside. As I lead them through the main rooms to the kitchen at the back, some of their mouths dropped open like the fish their fathers dragged up from the bottom of the sea. Others narrowed their eyes to gills. Jangmi, the girl who ate my lunch, the only one I could almost call a friend, wanted to know where my father hid his money. I shrugged and kept walking, the hunger chewing my stomach suddenly mixed with something else, something heavier.

"It's huge!"

We stood in the doorway to the kitchen, the largest room in my father's large house.

"How many people eat here? Your parents have only you and your sister!"

I shrugged again and tried to look at the room through their eyes. The huge woodstove taking up one whole wall, thick wooden tables standing in the center, crosshatched with knife wounds, cupboards stretching all the way up to the ceiling, stuffed with shushing sacks of grain and rainbow jars of pickles, stacked with salt and spices. Baskets hanging from the ceiling coddled fresh vegetables and fruit, out of reach of the mice who lived in the walls.

Out of the reach of small children, too. At least until that moment.

My classmates stood crowded in the doorway.

"Are you sure we're allowed in here?"

I squared my shoulders and marched up to the stove, taking a log from the floor and thrusting it into the mouth of the beast. Sparks shot towards the blackened ceiling, but I made myself face the heat.

"It's my kitchen." I clasped my own elbows to hold myself together. "I'll show you."

I unlaced the ropes from the hooks on the walls and two of us lowered the baskets to the floor. We lifted out round grandfather heads of cabbage, long red peppers like cats' claws, pickle jars packed with coiled anchovies. I showed them how to heat sesame oil in the pan without burning it, how to pound the rice for cakes, how to get the most flesh from the peppers, how to peel garlic so quickly it seemed to be taking off its own clothes. They were slow at first, their eyes round with fear, then with desire. The aroma seeped into the air and curled around their throats. I had them.

Jangmi was dishing rice into lacquered bowls, the floor around her spangled with dropped grains like snow, when I felt a fist close around my elbow. I glanced up with a sheepish smile, expecting to see Miha's mocking, scolding face. I wasn't prepared for the open hand that crashed like a wave over my warm cheek.

Jangmi dropped the bowl she was holding. The sound of skin on skin followed by the clatter of wood on wood.

Then silence crawled out from under the table, stretched, and filled the room. The other children looked up into my father's rigid face. I kept my eyes squeezed shut.

"Who told you to do this?" he roared. I kept silent. I had learned long ago that an answer only fueled his rage. His grip on my arm tightened until my skin was livid.

As he raised his hand again, I glanced up at my classmates through watery eyes. My father followed my gaze, and I felt his grip loosen. I could see their small, round faces overlaid with the faces of their fathers, the fisherman who drank in the streets, the laborers who chopped his wood and harvested his fields. He may not have cared for me, but he cared what those men thought of him. He let go of my arm and took a step back. I sagged into one of the tables, gripping one shaking hand with the other.

"I want you to eat every bit of this food." He pointed to the hot cast iron pan on the stove, where the peppers were beginning to burn. He swept his hand over the rice flurries on the floor. "Everything. I will not see one bite wasted."

He stood over us as we began to eat in silence. He watched as I crouched, scooped up the dropped rice and put it in my mouth, forcing it down around the lump in my throat. My eyes watered, but I dared not choke or make a sound. He waited until he saw me swallow and then stalked out of the kitchen, the heat of his anger blowing hotter than the flames in the stove.

We finished the food in silence. Sunyi appeared, her mouth a line of disapproval. She gathered up the knives, the bowls, the pans on the stove, piling everything in the deep sink. With her eyes she sent me to fetch water to boil for cleaning. The other children slipped out through the back door, not daring to set foot in the house, where my father seethed and boiled. None of them thanked me. I didn't expect them to.

That night, I was excluded from dinner with my sister and the maids. I lay facedown on my futon on the floor, sick with the smell of pickled fish. I waited for Sunyi to come light the candle in my room. I hoped my sister would find a way to sneak in to comfort me. But no one came to lift the darkness. I drifted as the nighttime sounds of the house crept into the corners of my room.

Suddenly, I jerked out of sleep to the rough tread of my father's feet across the floor. He came quickly, hefting something shadowy in his hand. It wasn't until it connected with my spine that I recognized the cast iron pan from the stove, chilled now with the darkness of night. It scythed the air, pursued by my father's grunts as he raised the heavy metal and brought it down on my back over and over again. I used my thin pillow to stifle my screams.

After that night, I spent months lying flat on that floor, unable to stand. My father did not consider me worthy of a trip to the hospital. Instead, Sunyi brought me bitter potions of herbs from the local healer. I spit their medicine into my chamber pot. My sister dribbled soup into my mouth. My spine protruded like a mountain range from the pale skin on my back as I grew thinner. Miha pleaded with me. She shed tears over my broken body, told me she was sorry she hadn't been able to protect me. She vowed to take care of me in the future, if I would only get well. If I would only stay in this world and not leave her alone.

I had to learn to walk all over again, stumbling through the house like a toddler, clinging to walls and furniture. My shoulders tilted over my damaged spine, and my twisted right leg would not bear my weight. It dragged behind my left, and I moved like a small boat in a storm-tossed sea. When I finally returned to school, the other children avoided my gaze. They continued to eat the food I brought for lunch. It all crumbled like sand in my mouth. I was nothing but skin wrapped around the stone filling me up inside. But for a while, they stopped calling me names. In fact, they stopped talking to me at all.

The pain of that beating lived behind my eyes and in my damaged limbs. It was constant, even in sleep. I sometimes dreamt that my skeleton had pierced my skin, that everyone could see the mess of bent bones I'd inherited from my father's rage. I feared that soon I would be nothing but a poorly healed wound. A scar, thick and ghostlike. But harder to cleave.

After that day, I often fantasized about what life would have been like if I'd been an orphan, alone in the world with Miha. There was a small house in our town devoted to the care of war orphans. I imagined a narrow, neat futon in a room next to a dozen others. I imagined gathering around the fire in the stove with children my own age. I imagined what it would be like to give one of them my suffering to carry, and to carry theirs in return. Every day on my way to school, I passed that building, and one piercing winter morning I finally summoned the courage to go inside. The woman boiling the water for the children's breakfast sent me to wait in the hall, where another woman, severe and stoop-shouldered, with a wide silver streak in her hair, swept in through the open door and tilted one ear towards me to hear my tale. She cut me off with a whip of her hand.

"But you have parents. This place is for children who have no one."

I protested. Abandonment would be better than neglect.

"Such ingratitude! With all of your privileges. With all the generosity your father shows to the people of this town. You bring shame to his house."

It wasn't the first or the last time an adult echoed my father's opinion of me. Whether they really believed I deserved his treatment, I'll never know. When he heard about my trip to the orphanage, he locked me out of the house and left me to freeze through the night, huddled next to the chimney for warmth. I drifted into a fitful sleep, lulled by the false heat that gradually spread through my hands and feet. I woke to find a snake curled against the rough stone next to my thigh. But I was too cold to jump up, or even to scream. I swallowed my panic and let it sit, wrapped up tight in my lungs. I realized that the snake had learned to adapt to his environment. He knew how to find warmth without anybody giving it to him. I would also have to rely on myself. That morning, something inside me sat up and looked out at a world that was hostile, but mine.

Up until the cooking lesson, my father had contented himself with echoing my stepmother's words, with the occasional slap. But something about me leading the town children into his kitchen, wearing my mother's face, claiming his space and his food as mine, had turned up the heat on his resentment. After my trip to the orphanage, it boiled over. At that time, my uncle and his family lived across the street. My father's abuse was an open secret, all the more so after I'd told my story to the caretaker at the orphanage. Later I understood that my uncle had no power to intervene. My father was the older brother, and my uncle's wife and four children had depended on my father for money and food through the lean war years. I didn't expect him to save me. But I wondered why my cousins could move through the world without scars, without long sleeves to cover their bruises, while my sister and I could not.

By the time I was old enough to go to school, Miha had already completed all the education she would ever get. In my father's estimation, it wasn't worthwhile to educate girls beyond the basics. My sister's time was better spent at home, learning to cook and sew and manage the household. With these skills, along with my father's wealth and position, she would attract a good husband, and my father's shame would not be compounded by her failures as a wife. Her marriage would be arranged as soon as she turned eighteen. The sooner she went out from under my father's roof, the better.

So my sister was not there to pick me up and brush me off when the other children pushed me down. But she did her best to stand between me and my father's rage as long as she could. And when the time came, it was she who gave me a way out.

I have always had a knack for drawing. In my earliest memory, I sit in long soft grass at the knees of a tiny twisted torrey pine tree, drawing the face I see in its bark. On my first day of school, with more than fifty children sitting knee-to-knee, cross-legged on the floor, the teacher passed out paper and pencils and asked us each to draw a flower. As she wound through the room looking at our work, stepping over outstretched fingers and dodging bobbing heads, she took my drawing and held it up for the others to see.

"Children, look at this. Do you see? This is what a flower should look like."

From that moment on, I scrounged scraps of paper at every opportunity, drawing in the margins of the newspapers my father discarded after breakfast every morning, collecting the envelopes that showed up at our door concealing important papers with intricate red stamps. I'd take the letters to my father, wait for him to open them, and whisk the jagged envelopes away again. He thought

I was learning to wait on him, as a girl should do for her father. But it turned out to be an act of defiance.

Miha saw how I filled these scraps with images from my world, with visions and dreams and efforts to pin emotion to paper. When she married and I went to visit her at her new husband's home on the other side of town, she gave me fresh white sheets of paper to fill my time. Then, for my tenth birthday, she gave me my first paintbrush and my first box of paints.

My emotional reaction to painting in color was immediate. I tried every color there was, but the reds plucked at my sleeves and the blues pulled me under. These were the emotional colors of my world. I was submerged in colors and textures like seawater in sunlight. Once I started, I couldn't stop. The whirlpool inside me would swirl faster for days and then suddenly erupt into a waterspout, and I would have to find a way to escape to my sister's house and paint. I was beginning to learn that my own imperfections could be the perfect opportunity to convey meaning and beauty in abstract art.

Or in poetry. As soon as I learned to write, I began to write poetry. Words came to me in a rush, a frenetic vision of a world I longed to create. Stanzas took me on a journey. They showed me the depth and breadth of myself. When I exhausted my sister's supply of painting materials, I wrote poems instead.

I hid all of these early efforts from my father. My solitary life and the art I managed to make out of it cost him next to nothing, but he complained about my expenses nonetheless. At the time, there were no banks in my town. People like my father kept their money, their jewelry, their most important possessions in heavy wooden treasure chests, locked the deadbolt and hid the keys. I was one of the very few who knew where my father kept his key.

My classmate Jangmi hadn't forgotten my father's treasure chest. She was a needle-sharp girl with watchful eyes. Tall by the standards of our town, she curved her shoulders like a canoe. She still took the food I gave her, but it never seemed to fill her out. She only grew in one direction – up. Sometimes when she sat next to me in the schoolyard at lunch, she was silent. Other times she would finish the food and hand back the empty wooden boxes with a curled lip. She would pull down the left corner of her mouth and imitate my painful, uneven walk. She told me I would never find a husband. If she saw a fresh bruise or a red slash in my skin, she would tell stories about my mother's bizarre behavior, waiting for me to bite my lips and wipe my face blank. She knew where I was vulnerable. But she had a bully's instinct for how far she could go. She understood more than I ever suspected.

The other children continued to push me down, to pinch and hit me, to call me names. As we all grew older, they came up with much worse things than Solitary Stone. Jangmi waited. She watched. Then one day, when she saw I'd been strained to breaking, she told me how to make it stop.

Just a little money. A trifle, really. Something a man

like my father would never miss. I saw the logic. I had what they all thought they wanted. That difference had created a chasm between us. But the same thing that separated us could also be used to build a bridge. If I could only get to it.

I waited until my father was out of town for a few days on business. Until my stepmother was at one of the neighbor's houses for tea. Until Sunyi and the maids were busy scrubbing the kitchen. I unearthed his key and took two fistfuls of cash. Jangmi and several other tormentors waited outside among the pine trees. I distributed my findings among them, and they smiled, thanked me politely, and went home. The next day, I walked to school with my leather bag over my shoulder, my red watch around my wrist, and my head held high. Not one of my classmates harassed me. In fact, they seemed happy to see me. By the end of the day, I thought I had purchased my freedom. At least as far as school was concerned.

From the time of that first flower sketch, my teachers had nurtured my gift for drawing. They saw the determination, the focus that came when I was deep inside myself creating, and they conspired to save me. Once I started writing poetry as well, Mr. Kim took me under his wing. He let me stay after class and use the art supplies he kept locked away: pastels, colored pencils, charcoal. He praised every effort I made, and gave me advice to improve my technique. But he was most impressed by my poetry.

"Writing doesn't cost anything," he told me again and again. It was Mr. Kim who first sent off one of my poems to be entered in a regional contest. When I won, the whole school was invited to a special assembly, where I was to be one of the students presented with a shiny medal with my name printed on it. My classmates lined up in neat rows in the dusty schoolyard. Some of the other parents sat in chairs at the front, their spines straight with satisfaction. My father did not come.

I hid in the girls' bathroom, crying, all through that first awards ceremony. Over the years, that toilet stall would become the compartment in which I kept my pride. It was the first box I put myself in. Later, I let people put me in other, different boxes. But I did it first to myself. I'd hear the principal call my name, and I would make myself as small as I could. I learned to be humble. I learned that discovery and recognition were dangerous. So was being different.

Nevertheless, I continued to paint and to write. I had to. It was my only escape. My sister still supplied me with paints. She was pregnant with her first child, preparing to leave for Seoul with her husband. For as long as I could, I used her home as my studio.

When Mr. Kim wanted to enter one of my poems in a national competition, I knew just the one he should send. It was a naked poem, the emotion writhing over the surface of the paper in plain sight. I brought it to him at school early one morning, before the fog had lifted from the streets, when the sunlight diffused through the layer of cottonwool that wrapped us up at night and turned the whole world milky and opaque. Mr. Kim was impressed.

So much so that he didn't speak. He sat still at his desk, and I stood next to him, and we contemplated what I'd done. Black characters on white paper somehow created a mass of color and light. He rose and put a hand on my shoulder. He told me my writing would give me opportunities that none of my classmates could expect. My gift would save me.

That afternoon, I ran all the way home. It was my first national competition. I felt like I had one foot out of that small town already. I stopped at my sister's house to tell her the good news. That I was entering a prestigious poetry contest. That I would be noticed, invited to study in Seoul. That I would soon be free. She paused before the trunk she was packing and told me I would always be welcome to come and live with her. That she was proud of me.

I stepped through my father's door just as the sun was slipping into its mountain hammock for the night. Sunyi was carrying the empty tray back from my father's room. His peculiar brand of Confucian principle meant that women and men never ate together in his house. He and I had never shared a meal. He always ate first, at a separate table, in his own room. The women of the house would eat after he had finished, my stepmother in her own room, me in the kitchen with the maids.

When Sunyi saw me, she ducked her head and rushed out to the kitchen. My stepmother sat in the next room, staring at the opposite wall with a little smile. She didn't respond to my greeting. I turned to follow Sunyi to the kitchen. After such a long, exciting day, I was ravenous. That's when I saw it. My father's treasure chest, wallowing like a waterbuffalo in mud. The lid was open, the stacks of bills carefully arranged in a long line on the floor.

Frozen with fear, I waited. Silence wafted in from the kitchen. I longed for Sunyi. For one of the maids to come through the door and fetch me. I closed my eyes and concentrated so hard I squeezed a few tears out of the corners. Still no one came. The whisper and shush of slippers told me my stepmother had left the room.

No one was going to protect me. And I was willing to take the abuse as payment for the wonderful experience of helping myself and others at the same time. I was willing to pay the price. And beatings were nothing new. Neither was fear.

Then I heard his slow tread.

My father didn't say a single word. He waited for me to look up at him. My trembling lily of the valley head on its slender stalk of a neck must have told him everything he needed to know. He left the room and came back with thin copper wire, several long nails, a rope, and a bamboo stick. The stone in my chest had turned to ice. I was mercifully numb.

In silence, he tied me to a chair. He started by drilling the nail into my skin, up and down my body, concentrating on my wrists, the skin between my fingers, the backs of my knees. When I refused to speak or cry out, his face flushed red. He switched to the bamboo stick. I bit my lips until they bled, but my cries filled my lungs like water fills a vase, until I had to set them free. I thought they should have deafened my father, but the more I screamed, the more his face took on the contours of one of the stone dragons at the little temple in the forest. He looped the copper wire around my wrists and pulled until it bit my skin. He dragged me into the night, leading me like a prisoner in wire handcuffs. He pushed me down the steep steps, pulling me up with the wire whenever I stumbled. I thought he would take me to the ship, the one he'd bought during the war as an emergency escape, and leave me there overnight. The thought filled me with dread. Alone in the cold on the heaving sea. As we stood on the dock, as I bent double with pain, staring down at my bare feet, he spoke for the first time.

"Do you want to die?"

I tilted my head up, but I knew better than to meet his gaze. I couldn't find the hatred in his voice, the contempt I was so used to hearing. He sounded curious, as if he really wanted to know the answer. But long experience had taught me never to respond. I focused on a welt of blood on my big toe, where the sharp nail had gone especially deep. With dry eyes, I watched it well up and drip like a tear. He tugged at the end of the wire, and my face closed in a wince. He asked me again.

"Do you want me to kill you, or are you strong enough to do it?"

He never spoke my name. I turned my eyes to the rolling ocean, imagined sinking beneath the waves, growing colder until I no longer felt the pain. I'd seen thousands of glassy fish eyes, thousands of severed silver heads on the butcher blocks in the kitchen. I'd never envied them before.

Suddenly I was in the air, the water reaching up for my stiffening body. I broke through the surface, salt stinging the nail bites, the wire binding my wrists together. I churned the water with my pierced feet, all thoughts of death wiped away by the shock of that black ocean. On the dock, my father had already turned his back. On the beach, a white ghostlike figure suddenly brought my mother leaping to mind. I saw the water climbing her robes as she prayed to the full moon. I saw the light bobbing towards me over the waves.

In a voice that barely crested the roar, I told the ocean, "Yes, I want to die." And I stopped kicking.

Dawn broke over me in a familiar bed. The edges of my face pulled tight from the salt. I peeled my eyes open just enough to see through the fringe of my eyelashes. Cleansing tears drifted down my cheeks. A familiar face hovered over the floor nearby.

"So. You've come back to us."

It was my sister's house. She told me a neighboring fisherman had seen my father on the dock and heard me scream. I have no memory of calling out, but I also have no other explanation for my rescue. I think of my mother on the beach, and I wonder.

It was at this stage, the age of eleven, that I first learned that death was the core of life. Death was no stranger to our town. He came close behind the war, swaddled in outbreaks of measles and malaria, sailing on the typhoons that capsized boats and flooded the streets. I'd seen the dead faces of many people, of several neighbors and their children. Death struck me as a kind of quiet. I remember him as a white mask, all the feeling held fast under the surface. I dreamed of walking deep into the ocean. I dreamed of cold, flat, trackless sand under the moonlight. Death would have been the easiest path. Visions of emptiness were my faithful friends throughout my teenage years.

Death was no stranger to our house, either. He came in the form of the blowfish soup my father loved to eat. It was the one thing in our kitchen the maids were not allowed to prepare. Blowfish meat is delicious, a delicate luxury my father could afford, but the liver of a blowfish is poisonous. The fish has to be cut just right. One nick to the liver can poison a whole pot of soup and kill anyone who so much as tastes it. In Korea, there were stories of whole families committing suicide in this way. My father always insisted on cutting the blowfish and preparing the soup himself. My stepmother flatly refused to eat it. At the time, I assumed he was playing with my life, as he did in so many other ways. Now, I often wonder whether my father, like me, had his own death wish. Perhaps blowfish soup was his version of Russian roulette. A love for that soup may have been the only thing we had in common.

Once, when Miha came from Seoul to visit her husband's family, I told her about my death wish. She had left her first child, a son, with her mother-in-law and come to see me. We were sitting on our father's porch, wrapped in the summer evening, listening to Sunyi and the other maids shriek with laughter as they scrubbed the pots in the kitchen. The breeze off the sea smelled of warmth and light.

I had never voiced my emotion so openly to anyone. My sister turned a solemn face on me, and I reached down to pick at the constellation of scars running down my bare calf. Her eyes followed my fingers, then turned to the endless stretch of water before us.

"I see." She stood up, brushed the sand off her long linen skirt. "Okay, Hana. If you really want to die, let's do it together."

Before I could say a word, she was off and running. Panic-stricken without knowing why, I leapt to my feet in pursuit. She took the sloping road that ran from our house down to the beach. Her bare feet kicked up clouds of hot dry sand. I heard her howl as the first waves splashed against her knees. She leapt forward, arms raised to shoulder height, swinging, as wave after wave moved in to drench her. I caught up with her just as a huge wave took her in the chest. My fear of the water, of the boundless depths I'd felt tugging me down the night my father tossed me under the waves, rooted my feet in the shifting sand. But then Miha gasped and plunged forward. Without thinking, I leapt in after her, floundered until I caught something between my frantic fingers – an arm, a leg. I pulled with all my might, and suddenly her white face broke the surface, water trailing from her high cheek-bones like the prow of a fishing boat. She spit salt water and let me lead her to shore, faltering on my billowed leg. We collapsed high up on the dry sand, where the water couldn't reach us. I waited until her breathing returned to normal. I waited for my own body to stop trembling. I looked up and down the beach to see whether anyone had noticed this shameful display. We were alone.

She lay with one arm across her forehead, eyes closed against the setting sun. I watched her chest rise and fall.

"Sister."

She opened one eye and tilted her head towards me.

"I promise I will live if you will."

She smiled up at the sun and closed her eye again. I felt the stone in my chest split open, and something bright and precious spilled out.

I still thought about escape. But I stuffed down thoughts of suicide, ignored the pull of the waves. I was buoyed up by the hope that my sister's love was enough to keep me afloat. That Mr. Kim's support was enough to haul me out of the depths. They both told me that my only chance of escape was to go to university. What they didn't tell me was that there was no hope of my father supporting this plan. At the time I thought, if I was willing to go far away, that would be enough to convince my father. We were both drowning in his animosity.

I'd lived my entire life at a crossroads. I could see out

of town in two directions. One road led down to the sea, and the other wound through the forest and up into the hills, all the way to Seoul. I could see the path. But I had no idea what sort of vehicle might carry me a safe distance away.

In the end, it turned out to be a bus and my own two feet.

Chapter 2:
The Optimist's Anticipation

Promise
is an overrated declaration.

An optimist's anticipation
can't unify
a false dichotomy.

Vows
sell dreams and hopes,
capable of breaking
all the rules.

Perhaps
you can carry a talisman
against anticipation.

Till solace finds its way,
Condoling as it comes.

It took five hours, two buses, and a twenty-minute walk to arrive at the temple. Nestled in among the isolated mountain forests was a series of low buildings orbiting the main shrine where Buddha sat, patiently waiting to be exalted. It was a small sliver of civilization in what felt like a vast wilderness, carved directly out of the glades of blossoming cherry trees, cradled between trickling streams, washed in the gentle splash of waterfalls. As though human life, in this form, could be something more than a blight on the natural world.

My father had sold me into religious slavery. And I was pleased to be bought. For the price of a generous donation to the temple, he was now rid of a daughter who he thought could bring him nothing but shame. One whose strange artistic proclivities and physical deformity meant her prospects for marriage and the traditional idea of a good life were less than zero. Sending me to the temple was a socially acceptable way of getting rid of me. And no one was happier about it than I was.

As a female monastic led me past the central shrine, I couldn't help but be drawn into the joyful symmetry of the facade, the long tiles dripping down the roof in parallel lines, meeting bright red columns with ornate turquoise panels and intricate carvings. The temple bred serenity. Its geometry was a translation of Buddha's desire to incorporate heaven and earth. It was not the grand façade I had expected. Winding through this cautious splendor, I was led to one of the smaller buildings, where I was to learn the contours of my new life. My job would be to help in the kitchen, a fate I wasn't unhappy with. Cooking had remained one of my main forms of self-expression. I had left my paints and my pencils behind, but the life of a monk would be bearable if I could still dig channels for my creativity in my everyday life here.

I faced the prospect of every novice monastic without flinching. The woman who had met me at the inconspicuous gate on the pine-needled forest path, with her loose grey robe and her bald head, gently guided me to the starting point. Hard physical labor would push me through the membrane of this world and into the sort of enlightenment I would need in order to fully realize myself as a monk. I listened respectfully, but I had no real intention of following through. I had no religion. The prospect of Buddhist enlightenment failed to inspire me, certainly not in the way painting or poetry did. I was too young to be a true novice, something the rest of the community was acutely aware of. My father's money meant I was spared intrusive questions. The other monks respectfully skirted the issue.

As the woman in grey shaved off my long hair and wrapped me in a drab robe that matched her own, I felt the differences of sex and class slip like a heavy rucksack off my shoulders. I felt buoyed up. Any speck of vanity I might have clung to fell to the floor with the last silky skein of my hair. There were no mirrors in which I could see myself, no place for me to mourn the loss of my best feature, or to be reminded of my worst – my twisted leg, the tilt of my shoulders over my damaged spine. I was ready to patiently endure whatever this life held for me. Subject to such a regimented existence, so far from the place anyone but me would have called my home, I felt strangely free.

As she cinched the robe around my waist, the woman told me her story. She had been in love with a married man, and she believed he had loved her, but his wife had found them out. Shame came clinging to discovery's heels.

He left her with nothing, not even a token to remember him by. She had cloistered herself, shrinking from contact with the outside world. Within these temple walls, she had rediscovered her contentment, her smile. I thought of my mother and my sister, and I wondered why the world perpetrated such cruelty towards women. Yet I felt safe, here where my femininity was all but eliminated. Here where there was no chance of rejection, no chance that a man who claimed to love me could pull the rug from under my feet, could suck all the air out of the space in which I lived and moved and had my being.

My days were filled with a regimented schedule, cleaved tightly to ceremony. The stillness of the midnight mountain air was broken at three in the morning by the shimmer of the temple gong. Together with other monks of all sexes and classes, steps clogged with sleep, I would stumble numbly towards the main temple and join the uneven circle around the Buddha in all his golden splendor. We chanted as he looked down on us from atop his pale, peaceful lotus seat. Our chants clustered around the rhythmic beating of a drum, our voices flowing over and under each other, finally merging at the close of the prescribed hour. This was puja. A profound daily foundation for the rituals of banality that occupied the rest of my time.

Accepting the reality of my new life was never an issue. So far from my father's house, I relaxed almost immediately into the daily routines, the constant nipping hunger, the repetitive tasks. But I had a long way to go before I could even begin to feel peaceful contentment. I was so bundled up in the negative charges of my childhood, of the sea, of the hatred and fruitlessness of my small-town life. The concept of an enlightenment beyond the daily self-preservation I was practicing was as alien to me as the American soldiers I had run from as a child. But slowly, in silence, I built my own salvation. The noise, the violence, the roar of the ocean – all that was far away. Across and through my body, I felt the itch that accompanies healing wounds.

Thoughts of suicide began to recede like waves down the smooth, sloping sand. Death was still a constant companion, but his influence lived in my mind rather than my body. I absorbed the Buddhist teachings of detachment from the world as the path to enlightenment. My intuitive, experiential relationship with pain and death helped me embrace detachment as an alternative to hope. I all but gave up on finding a different path in life, but I also let go of the hopelessness that had so often driven me to the brink. The pain of abuse ceased to be part of my daily existence, and calm acceptance took its place.

I filled the space in my mind with an interest in Zen, which in turn calmed me and created more space. But I had no interest in nirvana. I struggled for months, kneeling painfully on my fishhooked leg, listening to the buzzing insects, feeling the flies crawl across the skin of my closed eyelids, before I finally learned to meditate. In the darkness of my own skull, I saw the dance of colors I had tried to capture on my canvases. There was a blue room deep inside me, a ladder I climbed down into a space I inhabited quietly, sitting cross-legged, drawing on the heightened sensual awareness that came with hearing nothing but the sound of my own breath, my own regular heartbeat.

It hit me all at once, like the bough of a pine tree snapping into place after some passing traveler bends it back. I discovered the power to search my own soul. To turn things over slowly and dispassionately in the light. Tentatively I prodded the tender places, the pain of my past, taking the first steps on a long and winding road that would lead me to the end of my life. I never found religion. Not in the way the other monks expected. Even at fifteen, I'd seen my mother's madness, I'd lived my father's debasement, and there was no spiritual break-through strong enough to convince me that any god wielded benevolent power. Not in my life.

So I cooked. I boiled rice and simmered soup, fried noodles and steamed vegetables, with earnest attention and no flourishes. Sustenance, not flavor, was the order of this order. With a teenager's stubborn intensity, I contin-ued to believe in pleasure, and I did my best to eke it from the meager ingredients my new life provided.

When I wasn't hauling water, cooking for the com-munity, or cleaning up after meals, I spent my time alone in my room reading. Students studying for the grueling university entrance exams were often sent to temples for weeks at a time so they could focus on their studies with-out distraction. The monks gladly accepted their parents' donations in exchange for room and board. When the time came to return to the outside world, most of these teenagers couldn't wait to leave. I collected everything they left behind and combed through this new information in the long, quiet nights. Geometry, chemistry, biology. I became fascinated with the workings of the brain. I read German, French, and Russian literature in translation. I recited Pushkin's poems on my walks around the temple grounds. But my favorite companions were the philosophers.

The tattered library at the temple was stacked with books on all kinds of religions and philosophies. During my last year in the town, I had consumed philosophy books while my classmates consumed comics. Mr. Kim had fed my interest with volumes from his own shelves. Those books informed my lens on life far more than Buddhist theology. They provided my stepping-stones to the far shore of confidence and self-worth. My father's Confucianism, with its insistence on the inherent inferiority and submissive nature of women, did not hold true to my experience. I thought Western philosophers understood better. I read Heidegger and Kant, Sartre and Camus, Descartes and Kierkegaard. But it was Nietzsche who seemed to understand my fifteen-year-old heart best. His books were like love letters to the battered soul-stone I carried around inside me.

Nietzsche believed that the creative life obscures the ugliness of the world, something I had experienced firsthand. I loved his poetic language. His thought seemed to me like an abstract painting. His ideas about the will to power and the death of God appealed to my childish naiveté. He knew that to live is to suffer, and to survive is to find some meaning in suffering. And it was through him that I discovered Lou Andreas-Salomé, who led me beyond Nietzsche's views to something entirely more open and independent.

Salomé was a prolific writer, a woman of diverse intellectual interests who cultivated relationships with Freud, Rilke, and Nietzsche. Her non-traditional approach to life and relationships fascinated me, gave me something to consider beyond the narrow confines of the society I'd grown up in. I idolized this modern woman. She reignited my hope, enabled me to dream again. I worshipped her in Buddha's stead.

As my new life steadily transformed from novelty to routine, I dreamed of a river running through a deep channel cut through dark stone. I became plagued by the idea that I would never escape this deepening chasm, never go to university. While the temple had felt like a refuge at first, I gradually realized that the longer I stayed, the more it became a cage. A trap. I was learning far more than I would have in my small-town school, and I was far more advanced than many of the older students who arrived at the temple to study. Still, I didn't stand much of a chance in the wider world. I was a girl, from an insignificant town, with a doubtful formal education. Although my father had money, wasting it on tuition for a girl would have seemed as ridiculous to him as it was beginning to seem to me, though for different reasons. With my background, I should have been a bargaining chip in the Korean national pastime of matchmaking, but my life so far had precluded even that possibility. As the cherry trees blossomed, bore fruit, then dropped it to rot on the ground, I saw my hopes plummeting, shriveling away to nothing.

Mr. Kim had first ignited the hope of university in my breast. Where that flame had once been capable of lighting a room, it now sputtered and flounced on a wick sinking into wet wax, but it hadn't yet died. I waited for a letter from him, at first impatiently, then with an increasing sense of claustrophobia, and finally with resignation. The letter never came. My path had been cut into the side of the hills above the temple. All things considered, it wasn't a bad way. I simply had to learn to turn my eyes from the tangerine sunset sky between the tops of the trees and focus on the pine needles fading to russet on the forest floor beneath my feet. This was my future. To nourish others in this silent, anonymous place. To pay for my small measure of freedom with obscurity. Some days I managed to convince myself it was not too high a price. The emotion that had once colored canvases climbed down the blue ladder into that hole I'd discovered inside myself. There I could be quiet. There I could breathe out my days.

Yet I was longing for color, for passion. I was used to standing out. When I first arrived, the anonymity of temple life had been a shield behind which I could hide the difference that had already earned me so much abusive attention. But as the months went by, I began to discover that standing out was an essential part of my identity. My mind was different, my art was different, and my appearance was undeniably different. And I realized I wanted to keep it that way. Yet here I was, an androgynous being in a grey world where the only color came from religion. So I read. I wrote. I cultivated my poetry. I pushed my mind into the molds of different philosophies. And I waited.

Months passed. The first frosts dazzled the hillside and made Buddha squint down from his leaf. My confidence bloomed as the leaves sailed down from the trees. The monks praised my cooking, my self-healing study of European philosophy, believing as they did that all paths to wisdom were good. The husk of a girl that had arrived at the gate that first day filled out into flesh, blood, and spirit. The flame inside me still burned, but low and broad, without direction. Then one ordinary day, Brian Albright arrived at the temple under a hard blue dome of sky.

Brian had also left the beaten path, which led from the doorstep of his father's mission church in the Korean countryside all the way to the evangelical missionary training center in Seoul. He'd stumbled and dropped his faith somewhere along the way, and in his search for something to pick up in its place, he wandered into our temple early one morning, in a dirty tie-dyed t-shirt and threadbare rope sandals, a blanket slung over his shoulders against the chill morning air. One of the monks brought him to me to be fed. At that point, the only language I knew was Korean. Brian had learned Korean at the missionary center in Seoul, an activity his father forced on him. It shocked me to hear my own language spoken so well out of a face that, apart from the long hair curling around his shoulders, looked just like those of the soldiers I remembered from my childhood.

"I guess I'm a seeker," he announced almost as soon as he sat down on a low stool in the kitchen. I studied him, my knife suspended in the air. He asked me what had brought me to the temple. He listened to the skeleton of my story as I chopped and sliced.

"Sounds like you're a seeker too."

Always reticent when it came to making eye contact, I turned and stared at his stubbly chin. It never would have occurred to me to refer to myself that way. I was seeking many things – forgetfulness and simplicity, singularity and independence, a university education and an artist's life. But I still hoped that one day my journey would end.

"I think I'd eventually like to arrive," I said to the vegetables as I turned my back on him.

Brian laughed the loud, brazen laugh I would come to know well. He lost no time taking the knife from my hand, chopping the vegetables in a haphazard way. His reckless onion wedges lay next to my orderly half-moons like an object lesson. He tossed the knife down on the battered cutting board.

"The best wisdom I know is that seeking is its own arrival."

We were both curious about the world. I could feel the heat in his big American laugh. My flame, which had a tendency to waver at the slightest breeze, took strength from his confidence. Brian told me that becoming a missionary would mean the loss of his essential self. I told him that Buddhist enlightenment would mean the same thing. He laughed and took my hand. He didn't disagree.

I learned that after he graduated from high school and his parents returned to the States on furlough, he abandoned his studies at the missionary training center and began to wander, sleeping in the open air or in barns and storehouses where he could, charming villagers out of whatever food they could spare with his wide grin and his surprisingly perfect Korean. Along the way, he'd spent a few days walking the country roads with one of the monks from our temple. He'd been invited to come to the temple and stay, to deepen his understanding of Buddhism and Korean culture. And now here he was. Taking my knife and telling me what to think.

His quintessential American brashness was startling but appealing. We were so different, and yet so much the same. They took his t-shirt and gave him a grey monk's robe, trimmed his long curls and scattered them in the courtyard for the birds to weave into their nests. Brian looked decidedly out of place dressed in the uniform of a monk, his golden hair framing his face like a halo. I was curious, intrigued to be a man's object of interest for the first time in my life, but also cautious, given what I'd seen of male treatment of women. Neither of us felt a thunder clap or saw a lightning bolt, but our mutual curiosity and our commonalities slowly pulled us into the same orbit.

Brian was the only one at the temple who pursued the mysterious reason why I had come to live there. I couldn't tell him outright because I didn't completely understand it myself. That only made him more curious. We agreed about many things: about the naiveté of a black-and-white world where everything was clearly and confidently bordered, about the danger parents posed to their children, about self-understanding as the basis for emancipation, about the murderous power of secrets. He was impressed by my knowledge and my artistic gifts. I was the first person he could talk to about the unraveling of his faith. I knew what unraveling felt like, and I understood what it meant to be trapped. I gave him hope. And he returned the gift. He tutored me in math and literature. He helped me study. He encouraged my dreams of university, of a life that would be mine. He presented the concrete possibility of a radical openness I had longed for but not yet found. In a few short weeks, I soaked him in like a thirsty sponge.

For months we talked every day, and often long into the night. The regulations at the temple were strict in many ways, yet in another sense, I'd never had so much freedom. No one checked to make sure I was in my bed at a certain hour. No one minded that Brian and I spent so much time alone. No one cared about appearances. I dodged Brian's probing personal questions and simply told him I was ineligible to marry. His eyes swept my face, and he didn't push further. Not long after, he told me that he felt it was his destiny to marry me. I was only fifteen, but I accepted his proposal as a drowning person clings to a lifeline. I liked him as a friend, one of my first, and I had no blueprint for what a happy relationship should look like. At the time, I had no idea what marriage would mean. But I recognized another opportunity to stand out, to do something different. To build the kind of wide-open life I craved. To cultivate the quintessential independence of the American girl. His blossoming love reflected back to me the color I'd been missing. When he told me I was beautiful just as I was, I began to realize that passion was something I could always find within myself, even when I couldn't see it in my circumstances or spread it across a canvas.

Brian dawdled at the temple. He had intended to leave at the first hint of spring, but when summer descended in earnest clouds of energetic mosquitoes, he was still there, sitting in the kitchen while I prepared meals, scrubbing the steps of the temple every afternoon. He taught me American slang. I learned to say "Holy shit!" and "God damn it!" He laughed every time I used one of his phrases, and I repeated them just to see his pleasure. "Holy shit!" as I scrubbed forest mushrooms. "God damn it!" when his sudsy pail tipped over the stone steps and soaked the hem of my robe.

He learned of my love for Nietzsche, and for my sixteenth birthday he gave me a translated copy of *Thus Spoke Zarathustra*. We discussed it on our long, slow walks through the hills. But we tumbled down different sides of the mountain when it came to Salomé. Nietzsche had asked her to marry him twice, and twice she had rejected him. I admired her intellect, revered her bravery, and glorified her open mind. I sung her praises to the twisted pine trees. Brian curled his lip.

"Well, I certainly hope you don't end up like her."

I stopped dead on the path.

"A seducer, a hedonist," he clarified.

"Independent, you mean?" I was angry.

He shook his head against my interpretation.

"My wife will be a different kind of woman."

We agreed on so much, but this disagreement was enough to stop me in my tracks.

"Then I wonder what kind of wife you see in me."

I left the trail and sat in the shade of a huge stone, the blazing heat radiating all around me. I shivered. Brian followed me and apologized, without understanding what for.

Despite our plans, it was an unanticipated future that came for each of us. When Brian's parents returned to Korea after a year away, they summoned him to discuss his plans. He told me he would return to Seoul long enough to assert his independence, to reject their plan for his life, to tell them about our engagement, and then he would come back for me. But somewhere along the way, another war stepped between us.

I waited a week, two weeks, increasingly desperate as I saw another chance of escape slipping through my fingers like water. When his letter finally came, it sucked the air from my lungs.

> Dearest Hana,
> I don't really know how to begin a letter like
> this. So I'll start by telling you that I've been
> drafted. Seems as soon as I gave up my plans
> for a missionary career, the government tracked
> me down. Or maybe my father sold me out.
> I wouldn't be surprised. He thinks this will
> be good for me. All I can see in my future is a
> tattered American flag, in flames.
> I've already passed the medical exam. There's
> nothing left to do but report for basic training.
> All I can ask you to do is wait. Wait for news,
> wait for me. I will be back for you.
> I'll write as soon as I know more.
> I love you.
> Brian

I shed tears, fewer than I would have expected. I wrote back to reassure him. Of course I would wait. Privately I thought, what choice did I have? Without the refining heat of Brian's presence, I slipped into a pleasant rhythm of work, reading, and writing, and found that it suited me.

After basic training and before shipping out to Vietnam, Brian was given three days' leave. Instead of visiting his parents, he came to our temple. He seemed to know that the war was bound to shake up all of his plans and leave them spilled across the floor. On his last day, he took me for one final walk through the woods. He hugged me close, whispered into my ear over and over. I remember the pressure of his arms, but not his words. My mind was elsewhere. I was beginning to understand. He might not make it back. And if he didn't, there was only a slim chance I would ever hear of his death. With him gone, what was I to do? University life bobbed to the surface again as my hope for the future. But what would happen if I failed?

I walked him to the temple gate in the watery dawn light. I didn't want to add my burdens to those he was already carrying. But he knew me well, even then. He pointed to the stump of a tree just outside the temple grounds.

"Look."

His gesture aimed my wandering gaze. The stump was old, washed by many rains, covered in orange moss. But it was surrounded by high green shoots, each hoping to grow into a tree.

"That stump looks dead. But see the seedlings all around it? The life force is still there. All it needs is water and sunlight. And it will grow. It's inevitable. It's fate."

I willed myself not to cry as I met his eyes, one of the few times I ever did such a thing.

"You've absorbed some Buddhist teaching after all."

He laughed his big, brazen laugh as he walked away.

Brian's refusal to absorb my doubts was the catalyst that helped me redouble my efforts. He gave me a plan and a purpose: to return to school, to forge the path alone if I had to. In the space of a few months, Brian had changed my life forever.

Once Brian was gone, I had to think of who to turn to. I would have to re-enroll in school. I couldn't expect a university to accept an underage monastic with no transcript, no entrance exam results. And I didn't yet realize I could simply walk away from the temple. I assumed that my father's gift had imprisoned me there, that the other monks were tasked with keeping me away from him, away from the town where I had grown up. And my father certainly saw my migration to the temple as a one-way trip.

But Mr. Kim had not forgotten me. And I knew he would understand my plight. I wrote and asked for help getting into university. He immediately sent me a long letter, relieved to know where I had ended up. He told me he had searched, but my father would not tell anyone where I had gone, only that I'd been sent to a monastery. Then he admonished me that it would be a terrible loss if my intelligence were wasted in an isolated temple. He urged me back to reality. He reminded me of the successes I'd already had, the contests I'd won. He offered to send me bus fare. He understood what it was to attempt to climb a slippery cliff with inexperienced hands and no guide rope.

I knew too much of life to deny the desperation Mr. Kim read between my words. He was my very last hand to hold. I had never confessed to him the details of my personal life, but he had read my pain in my poems time and time again. I wrote and told him I was ready to do whatever was necessary. True to his word, he tried to pave the way for my return to our town. But he was not able to talk me back into my father's house. My father wanted nothing more to do with me.

I wrote to my uncle. I asked him to intervene. I knew no one in the town could take me in against my father's wishes. It would be an offense, and no one, least of all my uncle, was willing to openly defy him. My father was indifferent to my freedom, and he would not help me achieve it. Not with money, not with space. But maybe I could wield his lack of interest, use it to secure independence for myself by promising to free him from responsibility.

More than a month passed before I heard from my uncle. Minutes and hours, days and weeks of wasted time. Every second at the temple had begun to seem intolerable. I had a vision of something more, something bigger, and no patience to wait. In the end, the Buddhist sensibility had not touched my core. When it finally came, my uncle's letter was formal and distant, informing me that my father had suffered a stroke, which left him almost completely incapacitated. He was unable to speak or move the left side of his body. I let the paper fall limp into my lap, imagining Sunyi and the other maids in the kitchen, whispering about karma. My uncle went on to say that any kind of mediation on my behalf was impossible with my father in his present condition. But then he threw me a lifeline. He advised me to write to my sister in Seoul.

By this time, Miha had four children, a son and three daughters. She had never had the chance to study, and she was bound to the traditional role her husband and his family expected her to fulfill. I knew she would have to ask his permission, that he would have to approve any decision she made. I dared not allow myself to hope. But I wrote to her to ask. Her answer came within a few days. Her husband would be happy to host me in his home. I would share a room with the girls and would be responsible for their care. In my spare time, I could study for the university entrance exams.

I jumped at the chance. Miha had enclosed a train ticket to Seoul. In the space of one day, I wrote to Mr. Kim and told him where I was going, changed into the clothes I had on when I entered the temple, and simply walked through the gate and back into the world.

In the overwhelming chaos of Seoul, my sister's new, regimented life filled me with a strange sense of trepidation. I saw the contentment strung loosely between her and her husband, and the taut love she had for her children. I asked myself whether this was something I should want. But then I watched her husband go off to an office at seven every morning and return well after eight at night, his salary comfortable but not generous, while Miha was occupied with caring for their children, with cooking and cleaning. I pictured them ten, fifteen, twenty years in the future, and the only difference in the channel of their days was the number of children and the shape of their own bodies. I saw what my future could have been, and for the first time, I was grateful to be different. It was a relief to realize I really didn't want the life that I had come to view as impossible for me. I was still somehow my mother's daughter. But I didn't want her life either.

I enrolled in a cram school in Seoul, and I continued to paint and write poetry. Once again, my sister provided me with paint, canvas, and brushes. I painted on the cinderblock terrace in the small garden behind her house, sweating out the last hot days of summer. I worked feverishly, in every spare moment I could find, sometimes long into the night, lit by the nauseous orange glow of the streetlights, surrounded by the hot-pink blossoms of her hibiscus plants. I had to pour out all the things that had fallen into the blue pit inside me during my time at the temple. I painted over the same canvas again and again, barely waiting for the paint to dry before I started over again, with some new emotion driving me, some other feeling I could no longer contain. The paint on the canvas grew so thick it began to flake off, little pieces of my soul littering that narrow strip of concrete, exposed to the sun, the sky, the wind. Little windows through the layers, revealing all the colors that had gone into the making of my freedom.

Mr. Kim wrote to me nearly every week, advising me to enter certain painting and poetry contests. I used up all my spare time entering every competition he pointed out to me. I enjoyed pushing myself to create things and to share my work, but with each entry I felt sick. I twitched under the pressure of the collective gaze of my audience like a fish on a line. I proved that I could win, that I could excel. But I wasn't accustomed to success. At times, I longed for the comfort of the old toilet cubicle at my little country school.

After months of cram school, after several more contests entered and won, my seventeenth birthday was approaching. Mr. Kim sent me a letter inviting me to visit him at my old school. He told me it was urgent. For weeks, I couldn't bring myself to respond to his letter. I knew I should visit my father, I should thank my uncle for his sound advice. But Seoul had breathed new life into me, and I was afraid of what a return to that stifling town would mean for the tenuous confidence I was building.

Late one mild spring night, while my sister's husband hunched over a plate of warmed up food at the kitchen table and we sat on the small garden terrace with tea, I confided in Miha about Mr. Kim's letter. She nodded, sipped, and sighed.

"You have to go, Hana." I dared not look at her. "It's the right thing to do."

She wrapped both hands around her warm cup and studied the paintings leaned up against the garden wall, waiting.

"The children should visit their grandparents. I could come with you." She must have seen the hope and the fear at war in my face. "But we will have to ask your brother-in-law."

Her husband, mild-mannered as ever, gave us permission to go the very next weekend.

My first sight of the sea in more than a year was suffocating. I felt the salt wind on my skin as I had the night I sailed out of my father's arms and into the water. Even the bright warmth of the early summer sunshine couldn't pierce the chill that descended on me. For the first time in my life, my father's house looked small, dwarfed by the wide open spaces of the temple and the tall buildings and fast-beating heart of Seoul. I walked into my uncle's house first, something I shouldn't have done. I owed my father the first visit. But what was customary and what I felt my father had earned were at war within me.

I went from my uncle's house straight to the school, where Mr. Kim was waiting for me in his classroom. The other students were just getting up to leave, collecting their books, and although they must have recognized me, they gave no sign, spoke not a word to me. Mr. Kim barely waited for the last of them to leave the room before bluntly informing me that my father could no longer prevent me from doing anything. He could withhold his money, of course, but apart from that, his power over me had been stretched to the breaking point during my stay at the temple, and finally snapped by his stroke. Without his sword hanging over my bent neck, the choice of what to do with my life was up to me. My future was in my hands. He delivered this speech pacing up and down the classroom while I stood, head bowed, eyes on the cluttered surface of his desk. Then, finally, he smiled at me.

"Someone else would like to see you."

He led me to the door of the principal's office and left me there, sweating and unprepared. I waited for what seemed like hours before the principal called me in. He invited me to be seated.

"I have carefully considered your chances," he informed me, shuffling through a neat stack of papers. I raised my eyes to his collar, and he must have understood my unvoiced question. "Of getting into a top university, of course."

I bowed my head.

"Based on Mr. Kim's reports and what I've seen of your coursework and exams, I am confident you have the necessary intelligence, and the drive to succeed." He studied the top of my bent head. "You are a rare student in the halls of our small school."

I bowed low and thanked him for the compliment. He drummed his fingers, heaved a sigh.

"But." The word rang against my ears like a gong, even though his voice was softer than before. "But there is still the difficult fact that you missed almost a year of school while you were at the monastery. And now, in Seoul." He opened his empty hands.

"Teacher." I was desperate to stop the construction of whatever obstacle he was about to put in my way. "I studied at the temple, too. Philosophy, literature, science. And I am enrolled in a cram school in Seoul."

"Yes." He bore my interruption patiently. "I am not questioning your ability. But under the circumstances, there is no way for you to graduate on time. This will look bad on your transcripts." He leaned forward to study me. "It will damage your chances."

My body began to fold in on itself, my shoulders hunched under the weight of this new burden. Without another word, he stood up and handed me an envelope with both hands. I bowed and thanked him without opening it, wondering what the end of all this might be. He escorted me out. I felt as if the wheels of my world had gone flat. A single pinprick was all it took to steal my momentum, put a stop to all forward motion.

I wandered back to Miha's in-laws' house with the envelope clutched in my fist. Alone in the room I shared with her during our visit, I opened the envelope and found several copies of a transcript, with the principal's signature and official red stamps. It was not my transcript, but it had my name on it. Classes I had never taken. Perfect grades I had not earned. A projected graduation date set for my eighteenth birthday. Less than a year away.

I had barely registered the shock of this when I looked

up to see Sunyi standing in the doorway. She smiled at me spontaneously and held her arms out for the briefest instant before letting them fall back against her wide hips. She sucked her full moon cheeks and spoke in a formal voice.

"Your honored father is expecting you."

The fear that invaded the calm indigo space I'd created within myself during my study of meditation was out of all proportion to my father's remaining power over me. Yet it paralyzed me momentarily. I could not answer her. Sunyi walked back down the street while I breathed deeply, forced myself to my feet to get washed and changed. My hands shook as I tied back my hair, which was regrowing and hung barely beyond my ears. I looked at myself in the narrow mirror over the ancient futon cabinet. I saw my mother looking back at me from the glass. For the first time in my life, her presence gave me strength. I thought of her, several doors away, eating her own simple meal of boiled rice and kimchi. The same kimchi the whole village came together to make each October and then buried in stone pots underground, to sustain us through the winter. I wondered what phase the moon was in. I asked myself whether I wanted to see her. There was no answer.

When I arrived, my father was already seated, propped up in a fort of cushions. I bowed to him in silence. Sunyi carried in a tray covered in small bowls of radish, fish, broth, noodles. The rich, familiar aromas filled my empty heart. While he ate, we didn't exchange a word. It was a long, slow process. The forceful, terrifying man I'd known was lost, imprisoned somewhere in this cracked, fragile shell. His will still commanded, but his body would no longer obey. His stroke had changed both of our lives forever.

I was numb, the old solitary stone stuck somewhere between my lungs and my stomach. I could not force any words around it. While I stood, waiting, I kept my eyes on the ornate wooden panels of the opposite wall. My father's gaze never left the side of my face. When he finally finished eating, he uttered a single word.

"No."

I had no idea what he thought he was negating. I searched the half-empty bowls scattered over the table. Sunyi entered the room to clear everything away, but he sent her away with a growl. I didn't dare question him, but his "No" hung in the air without context, without elaboration. I waited for him to go on. It hadn't yet occurred to me that he couldn't. His stroke had so debilitated him that a single word was all he could manage.

I could have tried to clarify. I could have asked questions, circled the issues until we closed in on the one he had his eye on, the latest thing he wanted to forbid me. Instead, I waited. I watched as his face grew red. I watched as his shriveled hands began to tremble. I saw the muscles in his neck move as he tried to form words, but he never opened his mouth, never let out a bleat that might have betrayed him, might have made him seem weak, less than he had been. I chose not to help him.

I had nothing to tell him. No word to say.

I turned and left my father's house as he struggled behind me, unable to stand on his own. As I stepped down off the porch and into the street, the ocean called to me. The sky was electric blue, the golden light of the sun just fading from the water at the horizon. I stood with the cold sand under my bare feet, my loose red linen robe floating in the tepid breeze, and I felt the stone drop deep into the hollow inside me. I heard it thud against the bottom.

That was the last time I ever saw my father.

It was the final piece that needed to fall into place. The next day, we took the train back to Seoul, the necessary transcripts tucked into my bag. By the time the cherry trees blossomed again, I had passed the entrance exams and was enrolled at the university, planning to double major in fine art and European philosophy.

Without my father presiding over my life, the octopus revived. I felt secure in myself. I was capable, talented. I had secured a scholarship. I could fill up the empty space inside me with skill and knowledge, with color and verse. And so, bit by bit, I took sideways steps up the steep slope of the mountain until the chasm below me was farther from my feet than the peak looming over my head. Then one day, I stood on the summit, staring down into the next valley of my life, awed by the view.

Through all of these changes, Brian and I maintained a strained written link, a sporadic series of letters shipped back and forth, a fragile chain that always felt like it might snap at any moment. He was persistent in his love for me. He never mentioned the war. The tone of his letters was always optimistic. He described the landscape and the people he met as if he were on vacation instead of belly-crawling through jungle terrain with a gun strapped to his back. He applied my favorite philosophical ideas to whatever topic he chose. His letters were long, as though he were trying to cram as much of his essence into the words as possible, to strengthen an already tenuous connection that was daily wearing thinner.

As the fighting wore on, it became increasingly difficult for him to get letters through. They ended up lost in a depot, or buried in the mud, or deep at the bottom of the sea, entombed in a sunken ship. I knew the general trend of his movements, as he was ordered first to Vietnam and then to Laos. But I had also grown accustomed to the long silences between letters. Sometimes I would go months without hearing from him. As the years wore on, I had come to depend on him less and less. I had begun to create my own options. I saw other opportunities for myself. His promises had taken on the sepia tint of old photographs. Our time at the temple faded into the past, a pleasant memory, proof that I could love and be loved. I thought it was enough.

So it was a shock to receive a long letter at the beginning of my final year at university, postmarked in California. He'd been wounded in action, his arm permanently twisted, his hand mangled. The government had informed his parents, but no one had contacted me. They sent him home to recover, and he had decided to take advantage of the GI Bill. He wanted to study philosophy at the University of California Berkley. He wanted to be a teacher. He would finish his degree and come back for me.

Throughout my final year of university, he spoke of marriage in every letter. He reminded me of the promises I had made five years ago, when I was still a child. I had not forgotten. But I made it clear to him that I wanted to finish my degree, that it was important to me not only for personal reasons, but for philosophical ones. He said he understood, that he admired my determination, my courage. He always had.

After years apart, Brain was more an idea than a real person in my life. I enjoyed his candid, personal letters in the same way I enjoyed reading the correspondence of my favorite literary figures, deciphering hidden meanings and references. But as the frequency of his letters increased, I didn't dissuade him. I continued to write, describing my studies, sending him poems and quotations. I don't know what I expected, but it was certainly not the news that arrived towards the end of my studies that year, announcing that he would be in Seoul a couple of weeks after I received the letter I was holding in my trembling hands.

It's impossible to look back and say what was right and what was wrong. There's no way to know what the consequences would have been if I had chosen differently.

Brian had so much to offer me. And he still wanted to marry me. I looked around at my options. I thought I would never again have a chance at a life like the one he was holding out to me.

If you let it, life offers a sea of white-capped choices. You just have to surrender to the flood of potential. The stress of making choices can cloud the water with confusion. It's often easier to bow under the wave of someone who seems to know better. Freedom comes at a high price. I thought of Lou Andreas-Salomé. I was too young to know whether to rely on my impulses, the feelings deep in my soul, or on careful contemplation. I felt my mother's red blood rising, and I did my best to tamp it down.

I never expected that Brian could give me a better happiness. I never imagined that happiness was something anyone could give me. The only certainty was that my feelings for him were absolutely new, something I had never expected to experience. We shared so much, and no one I knew, not even my sister, was so in tune with my perspective on the world, with what I wanted out of life. I was young, naïve, caught up in his enthusiasm for me, for the life we would build.

It wouldn't be long before I realized that the ideal we were both clinging to was next to impossible to grasp. Subject to the tides of change, our survival would depend on each of our individual ability to swim. There was no permanence, no security in the way we clutched at each other.

I always wondered what he was thinking when he decided I was the one he wanted to marry. Why take a risk on a young, vulnerable Korean girl? Why go to all that trouble to bring her to the United States? What was so special about me? Later I would learn that, as with most things, it was more about him all along.

Achieving the impossible dream of a university degree never quite felt real to me. Even all these years later, it seems like a story about someone else. I think my sister felt the reality of it more keenly and clearly than I ever did. She was determined to save us both, and she saw education as my path to independence and self-reliance. She was the only one who knew about my relationship with Brian. At my conservative all-girls university, boyfriends were not permitted. And at the time, I wasn't quite sure exactly what Brian was to me. More importantly, I knew my family would never accept him. An American, a fundamentalist Christian, a symbol of everything my traditional upbringing revolted against. Miha was not opposed to the relationship, but she made it clear that if I considered dropping out of school to be with him, I would have to forfeit her support and my place in her home. Her determination to educate her own daughters, to change the rules of the game for the next generation of women in Korea, inspired me even when my own future was clouded, hidden from my gaze. If there was anyone in my life I didn't want to disappoint, it was my sister.

Brian saved up enough money to come to Seoul to see me graduate. Miha was there too, with her four children seated in the row next to her. To validate the years of struggle and hard work that had begun when I was only ten years old, the first time I held a paintbrush in my hand. I looked out from the platform as I accepted my degree and thought I saw the future seated there before me, smiling on my behalf.

Brian and I spent two blissful weeks together. We wandered the streets of Seoul, showing each other favorite haunts. The city had changed even in the few years he had been away. I felt that it was mine to share with him. At his insistence, we traveled back to the temple where we had met. It was there that he reiterated his desire for me. And it was there, one night in his narrow bed, that we made love for the first time.

I thought back to the time we'd spent at the temple, and further back to my days in the village, with Jangmi and her taunts, with my stepmother's complaints about the impossibility of ever marrying me off. I had never expected to have a love affair, much less to have a man I admired fall head over heels in love with me.

He wanted me to come to the States to live with him. We would marry once I arrived. He would finish his degree while I studied English and explored San Francisco's budding art scene. We would hang out with the beatniks and the philosophers and the poets who were flocking to the city. We would have a wonderful time.

I agreed to consider it. I tried to hide my reluctance. If he noticed, he kept his disappointment well hidden. He described our future as if it were inevitable, as if it had already arrived. It was intoxicating, but I knew enough of life to be wary of such visions. I had begun to carve a path for myself in Korea. I had worked hard to take those first steps, and I wanted to keep going, to test myself against the limits of the possible. To see my nephew and nieces grow up. I loved the food, and the art, and the bursting creativity that was just beginning to take over Seoul. I loved Korean, the language of my poetry. Korea was the lens through which I saw my world and myself. The possibility of leaving everything behind for the unknown was exhilarating, but also terrifying. I felt as if the sea was creeping up the sand to grab me by the ankles and sweep me away once again.

I said goodbye to Brian at the airport. To this day, I'm not sure whether I really expected to see him again, or whether he really believed I would join him in America. But soon after he left, I started to feel weak. My knees gave out easily, and I had to lean against the wall on the landing whenever I climbed the stairs to the room I shared with my nieces. After a week of this, I started vomiting. I couldn't keep any food down. When I was still sick after another week, Miha sent me to the doctor for flu medication. Instead, the doctor performed a swift exam and cheerfully informed me that I was pregnant.

Shell-shocked, reeling under his hearty congratulations, I staggered into the bathroom at the clinic and vomited up what felt like everything inside me. I stared at my wan face in the mirror over the sink, propping myself up on shaking arms. The receptionist knocked on the door, offering anti-nausea medication and a cup of tea. She patted me on the shoulder, told me it would be fine. She didn't look at me when she said it.

I couldn't believe I'd been so clueless. Morning sickness, headaches, dizziness. I hadn't put the symptoms together. Was it willful ignorance? I thought of my latest painting sitting half-finished on my sister's terrace, covered with a tarp. I had just turned twenty-two. Unprepared and suddenly defeated. I was going to be a mother.

I wandered out of the doctor's office, into the city. The streets were warm on the side where the sun had touched them, cool where night still lurked in the shade of the tall buildings. I dove deep inside myself and came up with excitement. I was going to start a family. I would enter into a life I had assumed from a very young age would always be closed to me. I had been told so many times that I was worthless, that I would never marry, and now here I was, pregnant, with a man who loved me and wanted to marry me.

But this childhood dream was at war with another — the idea of becoming an artist, a painter, a poet. The joy of my own life. I felt the stone rise up into my throat, moved by the tide inside me. I told myself sternly that becoming a mother might be the best thing that ever happened to me. Brian and I could create our own little world with our child, shielded from the pain of both my childhood and his. I could go to America, start over again. It might be enough. When I stopped at a crosswalk, waiting for the light to change, an old woman reached out, laid her palm gently on my arm, and asked me why I was crying.

I urgently needed to talk to Brian. But when I got back to my sister's house, I had to wait for her to leave. I did not know how I would tell her, but at least I was sure that Brian needed to know first. When she left to go buy fish for dinner, I immediately dialed Brian's number. It was the middle of the night in California, and his voice came down the line infused with a kind of groggy terror. I could almost smell it. I gave him two words.

"I'm pregnant."

I don't know what I expected, but I certainly didn't expect him to laugh.

"Of course you are," he said.

His words seemed to puncture a balloon I'd been carrying around inside me. The sobs that burst out of me surprised us both. He sat silently, far off at the other end of the phone, with the ocean between us, waiting for me to calm myself.

"Aren't you happy?"

"Yes, yes of course, of course," I wiped my eyes on my sleeve. "But why now? Why so soon?"

"Well, what did you think would happen?"

It occurred to me that I seemed to be the only one who was surprised. I thought of the mornings we'd spent in his bed. I replayed the hours talking about our future. How he'd conveyed his fear of losing me, his dread of leaving me behind for the second time. How I'd reassured him over and over again. We were in love. We would marry. And no Korean man would look twice at me anyway.

"You can't stay there alone, Hana. Not with a baby. You need to come here. We need to be together."

My mind was still spinning through the alternatives. I ricocheted off Mr. Kim, my old principal. My uncle, my sister. All the people I would be letting down. I saw myself suspended in emerald green water, my limbs intertwined with Brian's, sinking as he clung to me. In eight weeks I would start to show. In twelve weeks I would be a cautionary tale. How easily the string attached to a woman's dreams can slip through her fingers, setting the heady helium balloon free to rise up into the heavens without her. But at that moment, I was still clutching the string, even as the weight of my pregnant body tethered me to earth.

I couldn't hide the news from my sister for long. We had become so attuned to each other after four years of living together that she knew something was wrong even before I did. Early the next morning, after her husband left for work, she sat me down and asked what was going on. I sobbed as I told her. She held both my hands until my tears dried on their own. Then she squeezed them and said simply, "You have to go. For your baby. He will have no future if you stay here."

I knew she was right. An unmarried woman with a

baby would bring shame on her family, but an unmarried woman with a Yanqui child would be ostracized from society completely. In America, at least my child would have a chance.

We agreed to keep my pregnancy a secret. But I would have to make plans quickly, arrange to leave before the reason for my emigration became obvious.

Brian knew very well that there was no way his parents would approve of our relationship. Koreans were objects to be evangelized, not subjects to be brought into the family. I suspected that conversion to their faith would be the easiest way to close the cultural distance between us. But when I brought it up during one of our phone calls, Brian was adamant that I should never be forced into anything. Perhaps he already knew that this gesture would never have been enough to win their acceptance. As it turned out, I became a convenient excuse for his own godlessness.

He didn't tell his parents about me, about our child. He didn't want to face their circular arguments about sin and guilt, about a mismatched yoke. Instead, he settled on the element of surprise. I trusted his instincts, secure in his love, in the knowledge that what bound us together was precisely the opposite of the family he had grown up in, just as it was for me. We had crashed together as we were each running away from something. It wasn't the best reason for a relationship, but it wasn't the worst either.

Brian's family wasn't our only problem. There was also

my father. For the man who always thought I was worthless, the fact that I was to marry, with no help from him or his wealth, would pale in comparison to the reality that the man I'd chosen was an American. My father, from within his conservative Confucianism, would look at Brian and see one of the foreigners who had invaded Korea with their guns, their violence, their religion, their modern ways. He would see the faces of the soldiers who marched through our village, sat on his porch, drank his rice wine, ate his fish, as if all of these things were theirs by right. But my father's failing health saved me from having to tell him about my impending marriage. He wasn't fit to receive the news, much less take action. And it never even crossed my mind to tell my mother.

It took three months to get a visa. Three months of waiting, enduring the shifting tides of fear and hope. I was going to have a life of my own, vastly different from anything I'd ever planned or expected. But it would not be entirely mine. It would belong to my baby, to my husband. To the new country waiting for me.

I spent my days taking care of my nephew and nieces, realizing now what those years of caring for them had prepared me for. I wandered the city, memorizing all the things I would soon leave behind. I read voraciously, leaping from one book to the next. I bought translations of Simone de Beauvoir and Gloria Steinem, Djuna Barnes and Audre Lorde. My mind began to resist the relentless march of my body. Miha made me the simple foods I loved, things I could keep down. The smell of meat turned my stomach. I dreamed of the fresh seafood we used to eat for breakfast, how we would pull sea cucumbers up from the water and eat them, raw and wriggling. I tried to repay her for decades of kindness. I washed the dishes. I watered her hibiscus plants.

When the day finally came, my sister saw me off at the airport, waving without smiling. Her children were there too, my nephew stoic and inscrutable, my nieces in tears, clutching each other's hands. I left Korea in a hot-pink A-line dress, one of my own creations, which camouflaged my expanding belly. My old red watch was strapped firmly around my wrist like a tether. The PanAm plane was practically empty. Such journeys were rare in those days. I sat alone, surrounded by wide, plush, empty seats. As we crossed the ocean, I saw all the richness of my former life stretched out below me, and I mourned. My mouth watered for the taste of grilled sardine, still wet with salt water. My nostrils filled with the smell of charcoal. I thought of my father's blowfish soup, of the death wish we had once shared. And I let myself feel the full force of the fear that I would never see my sister or Korea again.

As the sun set outside my porthole window, I pictured my sister's hibiscus. Lush with brilliant pink blossoms, living comfortably in a small concrete garden, looked after and cared for, but with no chance to establish roots. I thought of how such plants die just as easily from overwatering as from neglect. Or from a simple lack of sunlight. The desire for control is often what precipitates such deaths. And I wanted to grow. I wanted the density that comes with drought and the surge that comes with flood. I wanted to experience the wildness of life in all its complexity. I wanted adventure, and I was prepared to bleed for it. I wanted to cultivate resilience, to see how far I could go. And to taste all that, I had to leave the flavors of Korea behind.

As the plane circled San Francisco in preparation for landing, I checked my red-banded watch. Somewhere out over the Pacific, it had stopped.

Chapter 3:
Desolation

Hope has no fear.
It only knows
how to dream.

So the horrid disillusionment
of a regretful finale
topples the ivory tower.

No feeling left for
warm memories,
hopes or dreams.

But life still entertains us
with promises,
expects us to have a faith.

Perhaps
blissful enthusiasm
hears its own echoes.

It's watching his shorn locks hit the floor that does it. The guy in the mirror, the one with the buzz cut, seems like a cartoon version of himself. The comic-strip Brian. That's the moment his war really starts.

For five years, Hana holds the other end of his lifeline in her slender fingers. The letters he writes to her, descriptions of the world around him, leave out the blood and violence and death. He focuses on the trees and the stars and the simple kindnesses of fellow-sufferers. All that keeps him going. Almost sane.

After the war, when they meet at the airport in Seoul, he barely recognizes her. Her hair hangs around her hips, she wears bellbottoms and a white halter top, a tie-dye scarf wrapped around her head. The simple grey girl he remembers has grown a confidence that makes him feel unsure next to her. She looks just like a typical American girl. Like she's been waiting for the completion of her transformation. But the biggest difference is that she looks happy.

He takes her in his arms. She fingers his mangled hand. He asks if she's the Hana he used to know. Without speaking, she shakes her head.

They are strangers.

At the hotel, he loses no time asking if she wants to stay. Dressed like she is, it's easy to forget the traditional Korean culture she'd grown up in. But she stands up straighter, leans out of the hand he's placed on her narrow hip. He laughs, hoping to tease her out of her seriousness. She shakes her head, her long hair brushing the skin of the good arm he's rewrapped tight around her waist.

"You're going to be my wife," he tells her. "It's more than sex, it's about closeness. Openness."

A moment of silent consideration. Again she shakes her head.

"I waited for you. I can keep waiting. As long as it takes." He tilts her chin up until she looks at him. "I want to spend my life with you."

She hesitates, then folds into him, her head on his shoulder. He assumes the heat waving off her skin is a sign of release, of desire. But still she refuses to stay.

Hana doesn't smile much. The nerve damage on her face makes smiling difficult. And she learned early on never to do anything to draw attention to herself. So he looks for other signs of contentment. He learns to love the sound of her long, slow sighs, how she leans towards him when she speaks. The way she claps her hands when they've agreed on something. He sees her anew. She gives him what she can.

It takes a few days for them to get comfortable together again. He's patient. They're each different than the person the other remembers. She shows him the antique markets, where many of the dealers know her by name. They stroll through the familiar city like tourists, visiting museums, drinking in tea houses. He leads her on an adventure to rediscover the old haunts he remembers from his time at the missionary training center. But the market stalls and the street vendors he knows are long gone. The city shed its skin in the wake of the war. It is constantly in flux, with so many takeovers, so many assassinations.

He meets her sister, Miha, and her nieces and nephew. They are stiff around him, formal. He watches Hana cross the stage to collect her degree. He feels himself drowning in pride, his eyes swimming with it. But when Hana's sister closes her in an embrace, he feels the sting of something else, something sinister. He wants Hana to himself again.

It's Hana who suggests they return to the temple where they met. He takes this as a positive sign of her romanticism, the devotion of a girl to her first love. The monks are thrilled to see them, offer them a place to stay, although they make sure to give the couple separate rooms. The roofs, the trees, the Buddha on his lotus leaf all feel familiar, grounding. He knows by the way she curls into him on their long walks through the friendly hills that she feels comfortable and safe again. He asks her again to spend the night with him. This time, she agrees.

If she has pain, she never mentions it. They rise for puja and then return to bed. As temple guests, they are free to revel. They spend a week dreaming like this, coming together again, and any doubts he's had since their reunion are swept away by the rain on the stone courtyard at night. He is in love with the temple as much as he is in love with her. He wants her to marry him then and there, in that place, with the monks as their witnesses. She shakes her head, tells him there's no way a Buddhist monastery will agree to marry a couple of atheists, one of them a foreigner. But when he asks, the head monk is nonchalant. He says if both hearts are committed, then they're already married. Simple as that. Brian thinks it's beautiful.

Back in his hotel in the city, he unearths a Sears catalogue he brought from home. He flips it open across his knees. He wants Hana to pick out a wedding ring. But where he sees a symbol of their love and commitment, she sees comic photos of cheap diamonds, cheesy clichés.

She tells him she doesn't want a ring. She picks out a blue and red Mexican poncho instead.

He clings to her, to their plans for the future. He describes the modern, laid-back California lifestyle. The wide-open space in which she will be free. He tells stories of San Francisco, brimming with new ideas, art, and creativity. He assures her she'll never regret it. But she talks and talks about the dangers of rushing ahead, of letting things fall by the wayside for lack of restraint.

He sees her courage failing her just at the crucial moment. He thinks all she needs is a push. That's his job, as her future husband. He's the one she should come to for support, the one she should rely on when things get too difficult for her. It's his responsibility to save her. And the decision to follow him to the States is the first decision he will have to help her make.

He observes her carefully, staring out the window at the Seoul skyline, as if waiting for the city to give her an answer, and he suddenly realizes what he has to do. The box of condoms stays buried at the bottom of his suitcase.

They say goodbye at the airport a week later. He will go home for summer school. Hana will stay in Korea for the time being. Together they will decide when and how to bring her to America. He can't help but hear an unspoken 'if' under the surface somewhere, circling, like a shark.

He holds her close, promises to come back as soon as

the semester is over. He's comforted by her parting tears. Less afraid.

When the call comes two months later, he is not surprised by the news. But he is surprised at his own reaction. The receiver rattles in his hand. She tries to contain her emotion, her voice saturated and overflowing. He half expects the mouthpiece to start leaking the salty tears she pours down the line. Firmly, he tells her to get a grip. Get a ticket. Get on a plane. She needs to be with him, in America. This is the future she is destined for.

Only after he hangs up does he feel the full force of her wail coming down the line. It is a gamble, of course. He's pushed her to the brink of this decision. But he knows her well enough to know she will do the right thing. She will come. She has to.

A GI loan helps him secure an apartment. Even in San Francisco, property owners like renting to ex-military. Reliable, they think. Clean-cut. Brian's unwashed hair and huarache sandals don't put them off. He finds a place with a tiny boxroom, a narrow window, just wide enough for a crib. He buys a used sofa at the Salvation Army. A small table and two chairs. Playpen, stroller, crib. The only thing he buys new is a thick, luxurious mattress for Hana. He's saved his money to be able to give her one extravagant thing, a new bed, expensive linen. He wants her to be happy.

Then it's done, and there's just the waiting. The tension builds up in unexpected ways. The old dreams creep up on him in the night, and he jerks awake, panicked and sweating. His shoulder catches and grinds as he tosses and turns in bed. When he climbs the stairs to their fourth-floor apartment, carrying the canned spaghetti, milk, and hot dogs that sustain him, his damaged hand tingles, goes numb. He misses Hana's cooking, her calm self-command. He waits for letters, which come like clockwork every Friday, and he wishes for some burst of passion to move her to write on another day, to call in the middle of her night. The calls are expensive and rare, and when they do come, they are always carefully planned to take the time difference into account. He hears her voice only very early in the morning or late in the evening. He begins to associate the soft sounds of her carefully chosen words with exhaustion. The tension takes up residence in a corner of the tiny bedroom, under the window, and starts stealing his sleep. He lays awake at night, wondering if he's brought some malevolent presence into the house with the mattress, if some Han spirit is living in the coil of a boxspring. But in the milky morning fog, he can never summon the energy to throw it out. So the mattress stays. Sleep goes.

The speed with which the future barrels down on him seems at odds with the long days of waiting: waiting for letters, for exam results, for news. Hana's visa is taking too much time. He begins to suspect she hadn't applied right away, then that she hasn't applied at all. The hours of sleep he loses each night seem to guzzle his capacity for self-control, and his waking hours grow increasingly gaunt with worry. Some days he goes to class feeling as if the seams of his life are pulling apart like an overstuffed pillow. He needs Hana to hold him together.

As Brian's paranoia grows, it gets loud. He fills Hana's rounded silences with the sharp prods of questions that sometimes cross the border into accusation. She gives the same answers without variation, which either means she's telling the truth or that she's a good liar. Brian takes turns finding truth and lies hidden under the same words. As Christmas approaches, he alternates between scouring the antique shops in Richmond, searching for the perfect housewarming gift for Hana, and the overwhelming desire to shatter all the second-hand glassware in the kitchen against the exposed brick walls of the living room.

His mother calls. She wants him to come home for the holidays, to the flat snow-thickened fields, the watery lights of Christmas trees through iced windows, the night-time snowmobile excursions in puffs of moonlight and exhaust. She tells him his sister is coming. She tells him he doesn't have to come to church, though it would mean the world to her. Hana encourages him to go. He wishes she would tell him to stay put, to wait for her, that Nebraska is not his home anyway. Instead he has to tell himself these things, and then communicate them to his mother, who cries down the line at him. He is so tired of tears.

He celebrates the New Year in Chinatown, searching for glimpses of Hana in the faces around him, for some semblance of connection. For the first time since he was discharged from the army, he goes into a bar and orders a beer. Then another, and another. Drunk, he calls Hana, who has already entered 1973, and tells her he doesn't want to be stuck in the old year while his wife and child move ahead without him. She has never encountered Brian drunk before. Stunned, she sits with him on the phone until the fireworks over Presidio announce the arrival of her year in San Francisco. Then she congratulates him, hangs up.

The next time the phone rings, it spits out the news that her visa is ready, that she only has to go and collect it. She tells him she's on her way. He strains to find relief in her voice, or happiness, but the long-distance line thins her out into a copper wire, and all he hears is static. Six months pregnant, she boards a plane and crosses the ocean for the first time in her life.

At the airport, once again, Brian feels the strangeness of her. It's his first sight of her pregnant shape, her blunt sheared-off hair. He is prepared for another wave of insecurity. For the certainty of having made a mistake. Instead he's flooded with relief. He takes her in his arms, tells her how good it is to see her, and means it. She reaches for him through her exhaustion. Their joy is out of all proportion, a counterweight to the low-hanging tension of the last few months. His words unspool ahead of them, describing the apartment, the baby furniture, the bed, his classes, his plans to get a part-time job to earn some extra money once the baby comes. She lets him talk, nestled into the crook of his arm, dreaming.

The questions creep out of her the next day, between

her first view of the Golden Gate Bridge and her first taste of clam chowder.

"Do your parents know?"

His hand leaves her shoulder to point out an approaching trolley. She keeps her eyes on his unshaven chin. He sighs.

"I want to tell them in person."

Her lips try to convince her eyes to smile.

"With me waiting in the car outside?"

He points again, to sealions, to Alcatraz, to the Oakland Bay Bridge. He tries to inspire her to enthusiasm. But she pokes her uprooted fingers into the cracks between his words.

"How will I learn English? Can we afford lessons?"

He grins at the waiter and orders for her, his big voice filling all the space over their table.

"I'll teach you."

She pushes the bowl away, claiming cream makes her sick.

"Since when?"

"Since this." She points to the waxing moon bulge under her white linen shirt.

She stares through the window at the bay outside, at the small boats bobbing on the winter waves.

They marry in a blank room at the County Clerk's office. The witnesses are strangers, called in from the waiting room outside. Brian and Hana share happy tears. Hana dries his eyes with her handkerchief. As they step out of the office into cold winter sun, the future looks bright. They haven't yet discovered the darkness that inhabits the center of every light.

But Hana's first month in San Francisco leaves her unmoored. Brian does his best to give her time, but his full-time coursework and part-time job as a freelance writer fill his hours. He writes about Korea – travel advice, articles about Buddhist philosophy, commentary on political developments, stories about his time there. In different ways, they both miss the country of their birth. Their apartment fills up with her paintings, shipped from Korea before she left. Her days fill up with English white noise, punctuated by the nighttime crickets of Brian's typewriter. She spends most of her time alone, feeling sluggish, wrestling with pregnancy, with language. But the city fascinates her.

She wanders the streets, inspired by the markets, the flowers, the color. She gets to know the galleries, the Asian antique houses, stumbling through English conversations with the owners. Brian buys frames and canvas from a man in Haight Ashbury who repurposes wood discarded at construction sites, and Hana begins painting again. When the silence gets too heavy, or the roar of the ocean gets too loud, she takes the bus to Chinatown to buy Asian groceries, to cultivate some taste of home. There are very few Koreans in San Francisco, a fact that first surprised, then dismayed her. She quickly realizes that she will have to build her own world in this strange, enchanting city. Slowly, patiently, she is laying the foundations.

Early on, Brian warns her not to pick up the phone when he's out of the apartment. He reasons that she can't understand enough English to make it worthwhile anyway. But he comes home one day to find her stretched out in the empty bathtub, fully clothed, her face stony. Before she can explain, the phone shrills, sets his mother's voice loose in their apartment.

She and Hana speak different languages in more ways than one. While her husband learned enough Korean to preach, she hadn't bothered to learn enough to understand his sermons, knowing as she did that the content hadn't changed since she'd heard them from the unstained wooden pew at their clapboard church in Nebraska. Even during her husband's mission, she'd fled the Korean peninsula for the familiarity of her own community as often as she could. But she knows enough to understand that there is a woman living with Brian, that she is Korean, and that she claims to be his wife. His confirmation of these facts unleashes a tide of devastated floundering, followed by a resolve to visit him. Immediately. Him, not them. She never asks for Hana's name.

Brian forbids her to come. He only manages to keep her off the plane by promising to come to them for a visit. With Hana nearly seven months along, there isn't much time. He takes the opportunity of the long President's Day weekend and books two tickets.

Their first dinner together does not go well. Hana has

never eaten canned carrots and green beans, and she can barely swallow them. The sight of the roast beef afloat on a stagnant pond of its own blood, drowning in gravy made from its own fat, leaves her retching. Brian blames the pregnancy, but his mother is convinced this woman has brought some kind of disease into the country, that it's only a matter of time before she infects Brian too. She talks loudly, sharply, in barbed English words she knows Hana can't understand. Hana reads the content of the conversation in Brian's tight shoulders and pressed lips, in the way his weak arm trembles when he pushes himself up from the table.

His mother starts each morning of their visit with coffee and the announcement that it isn't too late to send Hana back. She jokes that the 60-day return period hasn't run out yet. Brian shields Hana from the details, but the emotion is impossible to distill. When they return to San Francisco, Brian's mother calls daily for updates on his progress back from the valley of the shadow of death.

Hana watches helplessly as Brian weathers this storm. His mother's anger is as relentless and wild as the waves in the bay. Hana has uprooted her whole life and crossed the ocean just so she can look at the same angry waves from the other side.

Each time she calls, Brian's mother has a new metaphor to throw at him. Hana is a doll, stiff-limbed and glassy-eyed, a toy Brian will grow bored with sooner or later and may as well return now. He howls down the phone. She threatens to call immigration. She says her son's child will be no grandchild of hers. In the end, he simply hangs up.

Hana's fear breaches the bulwark of her own body and floods the tiny room that will soon house their child. She had envisioned a solid, landlocked love, a clearly demarcated home, a wide network of support extending like strings of electric lights across the new country to which she has come. Instead, she feels the saltwater hate of her own childhood already submerging the baby who has yet to take his first breath.

But when that breath comes, in the wail of a healthy boy with round brown eyes and a crown of dark hair, it blows the fear out with it. Brian holds his son under Hana's contented gaze and sees the better half of himself, the best that both he and she have to offer the world.

He calls his mother to tell her the baby is here. That his name is David. That he is perfect. His mother hangs up, and for months the phone is silent. The tension uncurls, drifts out the window like smoke. When he holds his son, he forgets the pain in his arm. His sleep is deep and almost dreamless. For months, he manages to hold the storm at bay.

But the baby is hard because he is so soft. In their small apartment, Brian hears every wail in the night, every snuffle through the day, and the weight of it all builds, begins to press him down. He tries to study, tries to write, and fails. More and more often, he also fails to get out of bed in the morning. At first, going to class is his relief, the one thing that gets him out of the cramped, stuffy apartment. The one guilt-free excuse in his life. But one day it's just too hard. His arm throbs and twinges. He's too tired. He'll go tomorrow. But he doesn't. And he doesn't go the day after that.

Hana hovers in the doorway, the baby over her shoulder or attached to her breast, and watches him stare at the ceiling. She seems to be waiting for the rise and fall of his chest, checking to make sure he's still breathing. Sometimes he has to put his hand there, too, to see for himself. They hardly speak to each other. When Brian does get out of bed, it's to go to the corner store, to boil water for pasta, to spread peanut butter on bread. He stocks the fridge with beer, starts to drink with lunch, then instead of lunch. Hana tells him how her father hated drinking. He decides to interpret this as approval.

Then, like a typhoon building steadily to bursting, his mother and sister are there. In the hallway, on the doormat, arms crossed, looking daggers at the exhausted woman who opens the door. Brian hears his mother's voice even before she crosses the threshold. He rolls over, face turned towards the wall just inches from the edge of the bed. He hears her yelling, hears her stomp over Hana's quiet, barefoot tread. The baby wails. The fridge door opens, glass bottles rattling. His mother's shriek drowns out the newborn as she accuses Hana of alcoholism, of poisoning the baby she refuses to recognize as her grandson. Hana protests that she never touches a drop of alcohol. His mother lumbers down the hall, pushes open the bedroom door.

He expects recrimination. He expects I-told-you-so. He gets crooning, sympathy. Her hand on his forehead, in his hair. Just for a moment. Then Hana enters the room.

His mother attacks her. For making Brian sick with the awful Korean food she feeds him. For passing on some unspeakable sexual disease. For weakening him on purpose. Hana takes it all in without a word. Brian finds himself floating up towards the ceiling, watching from a distance, wondering how much she understands. How much he'll have to explain later.

His sister pushes past Hana in the doorway, hauls the suitcase off the top of the old listing wardrobe, unzips it, and begins to throw things in. All of Hana's belongings. She tears the drawers from the dresser and turns them over, pawing out anything that looks like it might belong to a woman – blouses, dresses, lingerie, jeans – and tossing it into the open maw. Hana leans against the doorjamb, her mouth dropping open. Brian's mother rises from the bed and leans close to Hana's face.

"You are leaving. Now! Get your kid, and get out of my son's house!"

Hana wavers but does not turn. She does not say a word. Brian can feel her searching for him even though her eyes never leave his mother's face.

"I brought him into the world." His mother is building towards crescendo. "I am his family. Not you!"

She huffs as if she's just climbed several flights of stairs. Hana does not step back. She does not blink.

Brian forces himself out of bed, like a tin soldier, one

stiff limb at a time. His mother rushes to him, tells him not to tire himself. Not to exert himself on behalf of this woman who is so far beneath him, so far below the standards he was raised to. She tells him he can do better. He will do better. He only has to send her back, start again.

Brian brushes her aside and reaches for Hana. She stands stiff in his embrace, her arms still folded across her chest. He maneuvers around her and down the hall, finds his son lying on his back in his crib, red faced and wailing. He lifts the baby as his mother appears in the doorway, arms raised, shaking her head.

"No, no, no. Put him down!" She leans on Brian's arm, tugs at the child, tries to take him. Brian squeezes him tighter, and his mother begins to claw at the baby. David screams. Hana appears in the doorway, eyes wide, one hand to her heart. Brian turns his body so that he stands between his mother and his son.

"Get out," he says in a quiet, trembling voice. "Now."

She begs. She castigates him for his sin, reminds him of the forgiveness God offers if he will only confess, if he will turn from his wicked ways. He can be saved if he repents. Sets his feet on a new path. Slowly, Brian sets the baby back in the crib, and Hana pushes past the other two women to reach her son. Brian stands between his families and points to the door.

"Out. I said get out. Right now."

His mother lists the punishments for sexual sin. For disobeying one's parents. Stoning, burning. Brian raises his palms, creates a blank space between them.

"I never want to see you here again."

As far as Hana knows, these are the last words Brian ever speaks to his mother.

Once the women have slammed the door behind them, Hana and Brian crumple to the kitchen floor and weep. The baby cries himself to hiccups, then to sleep. They hold each other through the night. Once the sun rises, they never speak of the incident again.

Sleep becomes Brian's only refuge. He envisions the vicious cycle of thoughts that plague his waking hours circling somewhere near the ceiling, like the mobile over his son's crib. If he just keeps his head on the pillow, he can separate himself from that whirlpool of guilt and reproach, anger and sadness. If he just stays horizontal, he can continue breathing.

Hana tries to pull him upright again. She tells him that if she managed to survive the tsunami of her father's anger, to get up over and over again, he too will survive this. Some days he despises the light she tries to shed, her tender, knowing eyes. Her courage embarrasses him. She tells him this is their chance to build their own family, their own reality. During the day, she transfers her vision onto her canvases. At night, she tries to hold him together.

Late one night, as she holds his hand atop the blankets and tells him another story from her childhood, he snaps.

"The difference between you and me is that before you came into my life, my parents loved me."

She holds perfectly still for one long, silent moment. Then she drops his hand, slips out of their bed. The bed he gave her as a gift, the bed he has claimed for himself alone. She goes to sleep in her son's room, wrapped in a thin blanket, wedged halfway under the crib.

The university sends letters enquiring about Brian's absence, asking why he hasn't paid his tuition. He knows the money is there, but he can't bring himself to write the check. He no longer sees the point. He carefully shreds each letter and buries the scraps in the kitchen trash. Finally, a letter arrives informing him that he is no longer enrolled. He doesn't tell Hana. He self-medicates with beer and whisky. He goes for meandering walks through the city, brings pills home from the park in little plastic bags. He loses himself in words and music. He listens to Dylan, reads Ginsberg. Some days he manages to feel neutral, but not happy. Never happy.

Hana complains that there is very little of the old Brian left. He tells her he's fine with that. He's found a new Brian. One without a past.

She begins to pour his beer down the sink, to flush the pills down the toilet. The neighbors complain about the music blaring at all hours of the night. Brian drags himself out to dark basement bars, open mic nights. Dark rooms crammed with men, tall and straight, short and round. He stands in the shadows, enveloped in clouds of cigarette smoke, and listens. Here he can press up against someone he'll never see again, who doesn't ask questions or call up memories, who's sweaty and soft for a few minutes, easy to pick up and put down again. Someone who knows where to score acid. Someone who holds him as he comes down. Someone who shows him how it could be.

But this isn't the future he wants for himself. He becomes obsessed with the dream of a commune. That wave has already crested and is long into its ebb, but he's sure that free love and fresh air are the answers to his problems. He sees a future Brian, slick with satisfied hope, long hair draped protectively over his shoulders again, surrounded by children who may be his own. He is convinced that the claustrophobia of the city, the isolation of the apartment, of life with Hana and David, has dragged him deep into this well. The light at the top is shaped like a sunflower. He shares his vision with Hana one night, after he's returned from another smoky club in the dark hour just before dawn. She tells him simply that her only home is with him. She doesn't smile. She doesn't touch him. But she agrees to follow him wherever he wants to go.

He sees it as freedom, traveling with his thumb stuck out, asking for what he needs from strangers each day. No money, no direction. No cage, he tells Hana. She laughs then, but there's a twist to her lips that he doesn't want to see.

Less than two months later, Brian bursts through the door of a large log cabin, set back from the winding two-lane coastal highway and surrounded by a thick grove of ferns and pine trees. The sun doesn't reach down into the clearing, and even during the day, they have to turn on the single bulbs that hang from the peaked ceilings. Silence drips from the fir trees, but they are not alone. Half a mile down the road is another family, a man and two women. He introduces each of them as his wife. Across the dirt track from them lives a woman who writes poetry on flat stones and shells she gathers on the beach. She sells her art in a lean-to by the side of the road. She lives with two little girls, who may be her daughters, whom she simply refers to as Faith and Hope.

Brian's disability payments go a long way in this small community. His arm hurts more each day, but beer and weed are both readily available to dull the pain. Rent is cheap, the forest is full of food, and when they come up short they simply don't turn the lights on. Hana grows thinner, but he likes her that way. His son has plenty to eat at his mother's breast. He has no plan for the future. He sees the horizon through a glass, dimly.

The pine-salted air dispels the damp predatory thoughts circling over his head. His mind clears again. He pictures his terrifying dreams trapped in the old apartment like abandoned birds, bashing themselves against the rain-spotted windows. They circle and wheel until they fall to the floor. Here, where the nighttime fog is thick and the sea pounds the cliffs to sand, his mind is free of eddies, his pain receding like the tide. The dam bursts.

Hana is cautiously pleased that their escape to the woods seems to have pulled Brian up towards the light. The stiffness in her shoulders loosens. Brian reads signs in the sway of her hips, in the face of the moon over the Pacific.

Big Sur turns out to be filled with just the sorts of people Brian had hoped to live among. Here, his marriage to a Korean woman never raises an eyebrow. There are far stranger things happening. No one seems to have a job, but no one seems to be seriously short on money, either. In this woodland setting, Hana is not the only Asian wife of an ex-soldier. Many in their small community are war veterans, damaged by both the violent scenes they've witnessed and the changing society they've returned to, moving out to the woods to live on GI benefits. Brian had never expected to become one of those guys, but he begins to see the appeal. He doesn't dare hope for healing. But at least here, he finds acceptance.

Hana is not easily shaken. She's read the Beat poets and the Bohemians, Henry Miller, Anaïs Nin. The radical politics and experimental approach to relationships intrigue her more than they surprise her. It's the self-destruction that shocks her. Alcohol, drugs, cigarettes, nonstop music, noise, and sex. And more than anything, the fact that Brian seems to slide gladly into this container. She assumed from the beginning that Big Sur was a temporary sanctuary, not a long-term solution. But Brian explodes every time she asks when he's going to return to school, when they're going back to San Francisco. She stops asking, but they both feel the question hanging between them the way their chain of letters used to do, taut and fraying, ready to snap and leave them adrift.

Yet there are also moments of perfect beauty, moments that revive his joy and send it whirling out before him. When he's sober and the money is running out, he and Hana go down to the beach and attempt to fish. They never catch so much as a crab, but the rush of activity, the cold salt spray, and the wind fill his sails and set him laughing, shouting, lifting her into the air. They stay up till dawn on the tilting front porches of different cabins up and down the road, drinking homemade liquor and discussing Kerouac and Ginsberg, Watts and Gleason, reading aloud from the Black Mountain Review. Materialism, sexual repression, spirituality – everything is up for debate. It's not exactly a commune, but to Brian it feels like a dream come to life. It's the gasp he needed to clear the air.

And David grows. He starts to smile, to hold his own head up, to roll over. Hana sets him on a blanket in the center of the bare wooden floor, and he begins to scoot around the room, exploring. Brian sits and watches his son for hours. But as the months pass and the boy grows, competition sets in. Even with the bare minimum of expenses, his son's flourishing needs begin to pull against the influence of his need for drugs to dim his pain. The older the boy gets, the less money there seems to be. He needs new clothes, semi-solid food, doctor's visits. Hana stands between them, quietly asking for more, and more frequently. His disability allowance will not be enough for a growing boy and a growing drug habit. He promises to go back to freelance writing, to become a journalist, to found a local newspaper. He promises these things in the morning and forgets them by the time the sun sets over the water. He dreams of mud and jungle steam, the smell of scum on stagnant water mixing with the scent of his own sweat in his nostrils even after he wakes. He feels himself falling, with or without the drugs. He dreads Hana's appearance in the morning, ghostlike, clean and white where he feels dirty, resolute just at the point where he is furious. But the pills take the guilt away and leave him with a sense of awe, the kind of distant wonder that keeps him tethered to his wife and son, holding his family at arm's length.

With Brian sinking again, Hana has only herself to rely on. She paints watercolors she sells to tourists at the local street market on weekends. She learns to make ceramic necklaces and earrings with stones she finds on the beach. Her customers include rich guests from the luxury Post Ranch Inn and spiritual seekers from Esalen. As her son grows and they need more money than she can make on the weekends, she begins to offer cooking classes. Brian watches as she plants both feet firmly in the ground of her new home, learning to support herself and her child. Like a young tree reaching through the canopy towards the sun, she is beginning to bend away from him.

One bright morning after she leaves the cabin, he opens the drawers of her small, neat dresser. He's searching for a piece of her light, her soft strength. He finds her crochet halter top, which stretches. A pair of stockings, which just barely distend to cover his thick legs. He stands before the mirror in profile, hiding his damaged arm, and stares. He's flooded with relief, like a festering wound lanced. His reflection provides an alternate reality where left is right. Then the door behind him opens.

Hana rushes in, searching for the wallet she forgot. Her shocked face reflects over his shoulder as her feet seem to stop all on their own, her shoulders rushing onward until she almost topples. He does not turn. She does not speak. Slowly, she backs out of the room. Softly, she closes the door. When she returns, long after dark, her top is back in the drawer, wedged in a dark corner. Her stockings are buried in the kitchen trash. Silently she makes pasta, steams vegetables. Silently they eat, lost in the contents of their plates. They never speak about what either of them saw in the mirror. Neither of them knows how.

But the final round of Brian's battle seems to have begun. He faces off against predatory pain, deepening depression. Gradually even the cabin's peaked roof begins to fill with dreams and visions, things he has tried so hard to banish every way he knows how. His mother is there, a shadow he cannot please, cannot inhabit, cannot escape. His pain is there too, in presences and absences. Of necessity, Hana is more out of the house than in it, and he is often alone with the ghosts. As they flit around him, he escapes outdoors. Sometimes he even sleeps under the pines in the yard or out on the cliffs overlooking the sea, where the steady pulse of the waves drowns out his own pounding heart. Only when he wakes under the open sky, whether shivering in the fog or lit by the first rays of the sun, does he feel he can breathe.

He returns to the cabin to eat, sometimes only once a day. At first, David cries when he leaves. Then he cries when he comes back. Hana begins taking her son with her wherever she goes, wound tight to her back in a long red scarf. Brian had loved her, married her, and brought her to San Francisco as part of an elaborate plan to save her. He hadn't realized how much he needed her, how much he needed saving. Now, as he watches her pull herself and her child up daily, he wonders whether she might be able to save him.

Late on that final night, he sits in the dark, waiting for Hana to come home. When she finally opens the unlocked door, framed by the lilac sunset, her forehead is prickled with sweat. David's cheerful round face peeks over her shoulder.

"S'about time," he mutters. She strips off the baby and sets him on the floor, pulls a wad of cash from her pocket and adds it to the stash in the empty flour canister on the shelf over the stove. She stands in front of him with her feet planted, wiping a hand across her brow. He avoids her tired gaze.

"What's for dinner?"

She opens her mouth to release something sharp, but thinks better of it.

"Just give me a minute."

She pulls cucumbers and cold soba noodles from the icebox, deftly removes the bones from a small piece of fish.

"Why don't we ever have normal stuff? Pizza? Hamburgers?"

She turns to him, the knife still clenched in her hand, her jaw working, and then turns away. He remembers the first time he saw her, in the kitchen at the temple, clutching another knife, a lifetime ago. He wants to pick a fight, to see her get angry, to prove something to himself. But he is tired. He sees her rising above him. He tries to remember how it felt to be the savior.

Over dinner, she tells him about her day. Sitting in the bright sun on a square of thin cloth, selling her hand-made jewelry to women whose ears were already dripping with emeralds, whose fingers were covered in gaudy diamonds. She describes their big cars and even bigger hair. She wonders aloud what Post Ranch Inn is like. What it would be like to go there. He snorts and says nothing. He cannot imagine a future which would find them reclining on the balcony of their private suite at a luxury hotel, overlooking the wide green Pacific. That may be in the cards for Hana, with her style, her talent, her perseverance. But it is not his life.

Ever since the dreams came back for him, she's been sleeping in a small room off the kitchen. There is barely enough room for a single bed, but she's used fabric and paint to transform it into a sanctuary. Late that night, he throws back the covers of the bed they used to share and creeps through the kitchen, pushing her door open on creaking hinges. The light cuts across half of her face. He sees her hair spread over the pillow, her leg twisted under the blanket, the way the California sun has turned her skin to gold. She looks so peaceful. Just before she opens her eyes, he wants to crawl into bed next to her, to feel the length of her strong, warm body. But when she startles awake and looks up at him with alarm, the desire crawls back inside him. Instead he tells her he needs to go out to the cliffs, to record the sunrise. She draws her eyebrows together and shakes her head. He insists.

"If I'm not there to record it, no one will. And it'll be lost. Forever."

The words make sense as they leave his lips. They seem to explain everything.

"Go if you have to go," she murmurs, her eyes lost in the darkness. In her tone he reads both exasperation and wonder that he'd bother to ask her at all. He's found his permission. As close to absolution as he is likely to get.

He looks around the kitchen and picks a notebook and pen up off the table. He takes a drawstring bag from the corner, the one Hana carries when she walks the two miles to the general store in Fernwood. He stuffs a jacket in it, and her old blue and red Mexican poncho, in case it gets cold. He opens the flour canister and takes out the last wad of bills. He doesn't bother counting. He strips off a ten-dollar bill and stuffs it back in. The rest goes in his pocket.

He stands before the closed door to the room where David slumbers. He pictures the boy, sprawled on his stomach, hair damp on his forehead, mouth open in sleep. But he doesn't open the door.

He takes a deep breath, holds it in his lungs as he wanders out into the starlit night. Somewhere in the hills at his back, the coyotes sing to the full moon, which casts his shadow before him on the pine-needled path. He exhales, thinking of the torrey pines at the temple. He hears the sound of the bell. The sea reaches for the feet of the cliffs before him, silvered by moonlight. He looks up and down the road running along the edge of the cliff, debating whether to cross, whether to turn right or left. Then he puts one foot out and starts walking.

Chapter 4:
When You Call Me Yellow, I Feel Blue

Even though
you do not know
who I am,
hug me my chimpanzee
sisters and brother.
Let us speak for each other
homogeneously.

Yet
when you call me yellow,
I feel blue.

Even
without a mirror,
I am always reminded of
Who I am.
A multicolored being.

Next time,
when you call me yellow,
I'll paint blue.

To this day, I have no idea where he is. There is no trace. He could be dead or alive, I know. But I take strength from the thought that he's out there somewhere.

When I woke up in the feathery green light of dawn, I listened. Silence. I tiptoed barefoot through the house to the bedroom. The door was ajar, the bed rumpled, cold.

Clearly Brian had never returned to the cabin. He must have stayed out all night on the cliffs. These short disappearances were nothing new. I got David out of bed, prepared oatmeal for him, tea for myself. I washed cups, bowls, the thin aluminum pot. These small daily tasks put a lid down tight on the anxiety creeping up through my chest. But when the sun reached its zenith and it was time for me to shop for my cooking class that night, I found that the fear had reached up and wrapped a cold tentacle around my neck. I had to know where he was.

I tied David to my back in his sling and went out to search. Up the road towards town, through the four intersecting streets that made up the village, then back down the two-lane highway. He was nowhere to be found. I asked everyone I met, but no one had seen him since yesterday. I gathered my courage and went out to the cliffs myself, scanning the rocks below, the battering waves, thinking every slick strand of seaweed might be a sign – a soaked poncho, a skein of his long hair. I shaded my eyes against the sun and took deep breaths through my nose, tasting salt. Nothing. A blank horizon of sea and sky. I crooned to David, who whimpered and sniffled against my thin shirt, feeling his warmth and even his tears as comfort, a physical presence anchoring me, even as the wind whipped at my clothes and pulled at my ankles. At least I had someone tying me to solid ground.

I walked back to town and used the payphone to call the county sheriff's office. The voice that came down the line was female, dull and flat. A man gone for twelve hours cannot be declared a missing person. That takes twenty-four hours. An entire day. I poured my worry down the line, his depression, his pain, his drug and alcohol abuse. She sighed and put me on hold. Then came a male voice, the sheriff, who needed to hear the whole story again. My voice was calm, though I could not control the tremor in my hands. He took pity on me and arrived in his black and white squad car a few minutes later, swaggering up to me where I sat on the curb in front of the general store. For three hours he combed the area, asked questions, knocked on doors, and followed me out to the cliffs, where I pointed to the places Brian usually haunted. Nothing. As we returned to the car, he turned to me with a practiced professional face and said the words I'd been dreading. Accident. Suicide. I didn't hear the sentences in between, just those two words, pounding against my eardrums and reverberating in my head like the crash of the waves a hundred feet below.

Fear paralyzed me. The sheriff's words closed the door on Brian's disappearance, leaving only the smallest crack for hope to creep through. He didn't seem to have much hope that Brian would simply turn up again. He'd been leaving slowly for months, in fits and starts, with every long silence, every alcohol-induced blackout, every bad trip. But the wave that rushed in on the ebb of that realization was bigger still, threatening to smash me to bits. The fear of what his desertion would mean for David and me. Living on pennies in the wilderness quickly began to seem like luxury compared to the visions that filled my mind. I had an infant son. I had no one in the entire United States of America I could call. At a push, I had enough money for a few months of rent and utilities. In twelve hours, my life had gone from precarious to downright hazardous. A riptide pulling me out to sea. I imagined losing David, imagined us both as orphans.

In the first few hours of the night, the fear threatened to swallow me whole. It was a tsunami, racing in high and wide and impossibly fast. But it receded just as quickly. My instinct for self-preservation swept in on the next tide. I didn't allow myself to feel, to see the scorching colors and the sharp contours of my own emotion. I let the next wave wash it all clean, and my vision of the future took on the monochrome of planning and facts. I blinked away my grief. The next morning, I smiled, I laughed, for the constant companion at my hip, and for myself as well. We both needed to know that everything would be alright. My stoicism would have to be the life preserver that kept myself and my son afloat.

I heard tires on gravel before the knock rattled the door. The sheriff had returned with paperwork, forms I had to fill out to file a missing person report. I read the fine print. After seven years, I would have the option to declare Brian legally dead. I balked, but I signed. The sheriff entertained David while I read, made faces and spoke to him in that strange nonsense language adults use with small children. David, who was used to me talking to him as I would talk to any other person, eyed the sheriff with suspicion. Taking the signed papers out to his cruiser, he turned to me once again.

"Call us right away if you see any sign or come across any clues as to his whereabouts. Or even if you think of some detail that might be useful. You never know." He lifted a hand, probably to rest it on my shoulder, but I flinched and he let it drop back to his side.

"You know, there are so many reasons people disappear. Let's try not to think the worst."

But something had stirred in my memory. I hesitated, the words pushing up against my teeth, then opened my mouth and let them spill. I told him Brian used to go down to the cliffs all the time to smoke weed and stare at the waves. But this morning I'd found his stash in the kitchen. He hadn't taken any marijuana with him. Where I'd been afraid this officer of the law would be stern about the illegal drugs stashed in my home, his focus was elsewhere.

"So he did something out of character. He changed his routine." He lowered his chin and looked me hard in the eyes. I held his gaze, clutched my son tighter to my chest. "Ma'am, that's not a good sign."

My neighbor Jack showed up not long after the sheriff turned onto the main road and sped away. I imagined him creeping through the trees, watching the menacing police car until it was gone. I offered him tea. He told me that somewhere between sixty and a hundred thousand people go missing in the United States every year. I wondered vaguely how he knew a statistic like that. He told me that if I had access to Brian's bank accounts, I'd be able to monitor any activity and know whether he was out there somewhere. He wished me luck, gave me the hollow reassurances that would come to characterize every personal exchange I had over the coming weeks. It may as well have been the slow drip of cold water on stone.

Alone again, I sat in the cabin and toyed with the idea that Brian had committed suicide. He'd certainly had good reasons. His mother. The constant pain in his arm, his hand. His depression. And of course, what I'd seen in the mirror that day I came back unexpectedly to retrieve my forgotten wallet. My husband, over six feet tall and two hundred pounds, dressed in my tiny halter top, my black stockings. His long hair pulled up in one of my tortoiseshell clips. Lipstick on his mouth, eyeliner blackening his eyes. I'd had no idea what to do with that image, what the implications might be. Maybe he married me to camouflage his desires. Or in an attempt to resolve them. Maybe this was a longstanding issue, or maybe that was the first time. The day after he disappeared, I still didn't know what to make of it all.

I knew Brian had suffered from his inability to protect himself, let alone his son, let alone me. Suicide seemed possible. But a simple disappearance was also something he might have chosen. Growing up, I'd wanted to run away from my own family so many times. I didn't have it in me to judge Brian. True misery looks to each change as a possible cure. The only goal is an end to the pain, by whatever means necessary. There is nothing more.

I still ache when it's cold or damp. A persistent reminder of pain. The sea took my childhood that night when my father threw me into its depths. Sometimes I wonder if it took Brian as well. If he's somewhere under the waves I see from the shore.

Other times, I like to think of Brian standing by the side of the road with his fantasy friend Kerouac, hair long and dusty, white teeth glowing against his tanned, lined skin, his thumb stuck up in a gesture of hope and approval. Begging and receiving the kind of freedom that can only be lived on the move. The image comforts me.

It is too easy to judge people who want to disappear. Most people cannot conceive of suicide in real terms, though most of us have thought about it at some point. Most of us can shrug it off. The lucky ones. There is no fault for those who sink rather than swim, just bad luck. Some suffering is too much to bear. I've known that misery. The forces of life and death were my constant companions from a very young age. Many times I would have chosen death over the continuation of pain. I could feel empathy, even complacency, in the face of Brian's disappearance. I could understand why he would do it.

I didn't question him. But I did question the nature of love. He had loved me so much, he had defied his parents and gone to so much trouble to bring me to America. It took me a long time to believe in that love. When he left me at the temple, when he returned to see me graduate, when I told him I was pregnant, even when I landed at the airport in San Francisco – under the surface lurked the constant expectation that he would desert me. It all seemed so unreal, so manufactured, a construction based more on his hopes and desires than on the reality of myself. But once we had endured our hardships – his family's rejection, his depression, the move to Big Sur, the struggle to survive financially – I began to rely on that feeling. The aftershock of his disappearance was the unraveling of that love. How could he go without saying goodbye? My heart froze and cracked around that question. His pain was one thing, but mine was another. Desertion sat in my stomach like the old stone that had lodged there in my childhood. It was easier to believe he'd slipped, or that he'd given in to a moment of total despair, that he'd lost the battle between will and instinct, than that he'd planned all this. My self-preservation depended on his split second of irresistible temptation. If he'd thought it through, where did that leave me?

But I pushed that question down deep into the blue pit I'd excavated at the temple. I shoved it under my grief and my fear and hoped it would drown there. It wasn't important, I told myself. Survival was important. My son was important. And I forced myself to focus on those things. The pit of despair would have to be cushioned with something before I could fall into it, and at that moment all I had was bare walls and floors and a thin skin of bills in my bank account. It would have to be enough.

Only once did I break. When I was sure David was

asleep, when the sobs pushed so hard against my lips that I thought I would drown if I didn't set them free. I lay on the cold floor like a broken thing, pouring torrents of water until I ran dry. I cried for Brian, for his struggle, for my failure to support him the way he needed, for my own vulnerability. Wrung out, I picked myself up with a word ringing in my head. Resilience. I found my poetry notebook and forced myself to write it down. More words came, and I collected them there in a manageable list, words that suggested emotional security, health, strength. I was twenty-four years old. I could handle this. I would move on. But where?

In America, more than ever before, my life was in my own hands. But only ever partially. Control was never complete. Another paradox I was learning to accept.

My experience of the United States when I first arrived was dominated by the phenomenon of human pigmentation. More specifically, how this becomes the primary symbol of race, culture, and identity. Perception changes according to circumstance, of course, and yet, even with this inherent chance for transformation, the color of our skin drives a fundamental judgment, a process of evaluation and division. In America, I was plagued with color-coded names thrown at me in the street. It was the first time I'd experienced what it meant to be a foreigner, defined by my appearance. I wondered if at bottom we really are just domesticated animals, dependent on our little name tags. My tag was indelibly written in the tone of my skin. I felt the heat of racial discrimination for the first time.

My uncle had tried to prepare me for this. Before I left Korea, he sent me a letter. He didn't know all the circumstances of my departure, but he knew I was going to America. He didn't raise any of the objections I'd anticipated, the ones I'd prepared answers for. Instead, he worried about what would happen when I stepped off the plane into life as a minority. He had traveled widely in his life. He had no illusions about the depth of the difficulties I'd be facing. But my father was still alive, and my uncle was not in a position to act in his place. No matter how clearly he could envision what was coming, he did his best to support me. And I made the decision to go. It was my choice. But no words could have prepared me for the reality.

Life on my own was a mix of fear and hope. Brian had shielded me somewhat. He had provided security, at first, but he also fenced me in. When I first arrived, I'd felt like I was wandering around in a dream. And after Brian disappeared, that feeling returned. My English was still poor, and I struggled to connect with the world around me. Big Sur offered fresh air, wide open time and space to breathe and reconnect. But without Brian, that space began to seem ominous. The lack of borders, of guideposts, frightened me. My vulnerability as a Korean woman, such a visible minority, began to seem dangerous. My dreams were dominated by the steady beating heart of the sea below our cabin. As I pushed the fear deeper inside myself, my painting dried up. The emotion I needed to convey, to spread over a canvas, in order to come to a deep knowledge of myself and my situation, was bottled and sealed. At the time, I thought this was the only way to survive.

Weeks passed in this increasingly arid desert. Then came a knock on the door that would change my life.

Brian still had a few friends left in San Francisco. Unbeknownst to me, he had kept in contact with one of them, a man named Jim. They'd served together in the army, and Jim had returned to San Francisco, where he worked as a lawyer. When Brian began to have trouble with his finances, when he'd struggled with addiction, Jim had tried to help. We'd never met, but when he heard from another friend that Brian was missing, he got in his car and drove all the way from San Francisco to the gravel road leading up to my front door. In Vietnam, they'd promised to take care of each other's families if anything happened to either of them. Even though they both made it back, Jim understood that return was an ongoing process, and he took his promises seriously.

I opened the door that day to find a small, whip-thin man with his face tinted red by the summer sun.

"Hana? I'm Jim." I gazed at this stranger silently, David balanced on my hip. He gestured at the room over my shoulder. "May I come in?"

I assumed he'd been sent from the police department

to follow up on some official business. I invited him in, offered him one of the small pastries I'd prepared as practice for a cooking lesson later that evening. They were still warm. Bouncing David on my knee, I waited for him to tell me who he was and why he was there. He gazed around the room as he ate, and for the first time, I saw my home through a stranger's eyes. The unstained floorboards covered with thin squares of cotton. The walls white and mostly bare, except for a few of my own paintings. The meager stacks of mismatched plates and glasses on their shelves in the kitchen. The huddle of half-finished canvases resting against the wall, as dried up and cast off as I felt.

He struggled with the words, licking his finger and picking every crumb of pastry from the plate before he spoke.

"I knew Brian. In the army. We were," he paused, eyes still on his plate, "close. I've been meaning to visit." He twisted his fingers into knots. "I'm so sorry."

I kept my face blank. He paused again, perhaps waiting for some sign of emotion – relief, or anger, or pain – but I offered nothing.

"I'd like to help you."

His words set off a wave deep in my belly. Whether it was hope or grief, I could no longer be sure.

Jim offered David and me a room in his townhouse. He lived with his partner, Ron, an opera singer who spent most of his time traveling. Jim said he wanted my company. He said there was plenty of space. He said he owed it to Brian. His friend, whom he loved. And so I went, without much deliberation, accepting help when it came, as I always had. Jim's kind, gentle support was the solid ground I needed to set me back on my feet.

Yet neither of us knew what to expect. The false cheeriness I exuded seemed to perplex him, but he never admonished me. He was there to talk or to sit with me in the silence. Most of all, he was there to take care of David when I needed some time off from my role as a mother. He gave me hints and suggestions, pointed out the path my future life might take. He had a light touch, but he wasn't about to let me flounder. He was the reminder I needed that I was not alone. He was the only person in the whole country who had my back, but it was enough.

I watched Jim struggle with his guilt. He felt he'd let Brian down before his disappearance. He didn't want to let him down afterwards. He wasn't a demonstrative man, but occasionally he'd stop and rest a hand on my shoulder, or take me by the arm and look into my eyes. He'd start to say, "Maybe if I'd been there." And I'd stop him. Partly because I knew what had happened to Brian was not his fault. Partly because I was afraid of discovering that their relationship had been something more than friendship. And partly because I couldn't stand the thought that it might have turned out differently. In order to keep treading the path before me, I had to believe that there were no other paths. And slowly, step by careful step, my false cheer became genuine.

Our friendship quickly sprouted and grew from the

seeds our mutual love for Brian had planted. He offered to support me if I wanted to go back to school. I hesitated. I worried about my English, about the barriers I would face. And I worried about my son. I needed a solution that would allow me to support him, and soon. I had learned the hard way that depending on a man, regardless of the relationship, was not a solid foundation on which to build my future. But I couldn't see another path. Luckily Jim could.

He came home one day laden with fresh fish, bean sprouts, and spinach, and he told me there was a shop for rent around the corner. I stared. I had no experience running a shop, and I had nothing to sell. Jim had the answer. Asian antiques. The life-blood of the San Francisco art market. It was a simple business to get off the ground. With my artist's eye and my connections to the art world in Korea, with his money to pay the rent, he saw it as a natural progression. But I didn't want a loan, and I didn't want to rely on Jim's money. As he talked, a different path unfolded in my imagination. A consignment shop specializing in Asian antiques and art would be much easier than selling merchandise I had to pay for in advance. I pictured the markets Brian and I had wandered through together in Seoul, what seemed like lifetimes ago. I knew I could find the kinds of unique objects that would sell. But the bottom line was that I had no idea how to run a business. I knew just enough to know that most new businesses fail.

So we compromised. I borrowed enough from Jim to

cover a few months' rent. I placed ads in local newspapers. And I waited. To my surprise, I was inundated with responses. Plenty of people had objects they were eager to get off their hands. In the space of just a few weeks, the small room with its brick façade and huge plate-glass window was completely filled with fine porcelain, subtle paintings, elaborate jade carvings, intricate wooden screens, beautiful dark furniture, stacks of oriental carpets, Japanese block prints, and a large wooden chest that reminded me of my father and caused a small tremor in my heart whenever I passed it.

I was inspired. To be surrounded by truly great workmanship, the craft of unknown artists from the past. I felt I was part of a conversation that closed the distance of space and time between my past and my future. I started painting again. Quietly, at night, when David was asleep and Jim was out with friends or busy in his office. I never showed my work to him. If he noticed the smell of oil paint and turpentine seeping from under the door of my room, he never said a word.

The beautiful objects in the shop started to sell. Each time I wrapped a piece carefully in plastic or cotton wool, each time I helped a customer load a gorgeous lacquered cabinet into the back of a truck, I felt a mixture of pride and remorse, the solid feeling of my own strong back and arms mingled with a pang of sadness over parting with something I felt such a strong connection to. I imagined these pieces in houses and offices all over the city, gathering memories, and I felt part of their journey.

By this point, I was accustomed to haggling. A consignment shop seems to invite it even more than other antique shops. Customers expect to get something for practically nothing. I'd learned to insist on the value of the objects in my shop, not so much for my own benefit, but because I felt the objects themselves deserved it. They had worth that was not negotiable.

From time to time, as my confidence grew, I went to local auction houses. First I sold some of the objects from my shop, and as I started to earn more money than I needed, I increasingly took to buying up things that caught my eye. I was learning which pieces would be most profitable and easiest to sell. I met other antiques dealers, interior decorators, and collectors, and I began to feel like I was part of this crowd. I still kept largely to myself, but the mere fact of having acquaintances I could smile at, stand next to, and talk business with provided a kind of contact and confidence I needed in those days. It was a sign of success.

My shop was a peaceful spot in the bustling city, with people browsing silently, occasionally turning to me with questions. I came to think of it as a space similar to a temple, where the objects took on sacred qualities and the art inspired awe and tranquility. But the auction houses were something else. Loud and crowded with interesting faces, interesting stories. After business was done, we found time to talk about antiques, art, and life.

David also flourished during this time. Jim was a very present father figure in a way that Brian had never been able to be. Brian loved his son, but too many other things got in the way. Jim, who had no opportunity to have children of his own, treated David like a precious magical object that had arrived in his home, as if it was all too good to be true. David adored him. After Brian's disappearance, David quickly adjusted to life in San Francisco. He was a quiet child, slow to learn to speak, and Brian disappeared just after his first birthday, so David never learned to say Daddy. Instead, he learned to call for Jim. It broke my heart even as I smiled at how happy they were together.

In the beginning, I took David with me to the shop, but as I started spending more time at the auction houses and antique markets, and as David started learning to walk, I had to find another solution. Jim helped me find a nanny who came to the house during the day and stayed with David when I went out. In the evenings, we'd cook together. Jim would tell me about his work in the county prosecutor's office, and I'd describe the objects I'd bought and sold. It was not the life or the family I'd pictured when I got on that plane and left Korea, but it was a family all the same.

As I grew comfortable and settled on this new path, I was reminded that happiness is attractive. Some of my clients spent more time in the shop than others. They wanted to sit with me and discuss the historical significance of Japanese block prints or the provenance of certain painted porcelain. Some of the other dealers wanted to buy me a drink after the auctions. Sometimes flowers would arrive at the shop with a thank-you card and a phone number. Other times a car would pull up to the curb just as I was locking the door, and I'd be asked to dinner. I accepted these gestures gratefully, but continued to refuse firmly. I had a business to run, a young son who needed my attention. And although my heart was healing, the scars were still red and raw.

Within a year of returning to San Francisco, I had paid off my debt to Jim and was growing tired of the life of a shopkeeper. I was restless. I couldn't see myself linked to one place my entire life. I wanted freedom, and I wanted work that was dynamic and creative. I sold the consignment business and invested the money into wholesale antique imports. I rented space in a larger warehouse, with Jim as my investor. This meant traveling around Asia on a buying trip. It was the first time since leaving Korea that I'd been more than two hundred miles from San Francisco. The three weeks I spent snapping up fascinating art objects across Japan, Hong Kong, Thailand, and Korea hit me like a wind roaring inland off the sea. For the first time in more than two years, I was not a wife, not a mother, and when I touched down in Seoul, not even a foreigner. I felt real freedom for the first time in my life. It was the kind of feeling I had dreamed of as a child, and had thought I could find only in disappearance or even death. Now I was returning with a whole new horizon stretched out before me.

Yet it was not a homecoming. I could not think of Korea as my home. It was too complicated for simple feelings of cheerful familiarity and warm security. I relished the food, and the language. I ate until I couldn't take another bite, and I talked more in two days than I had in two months. The familiar vendors at the art market greeted me like a long-lost friend. Everyone told me how happy I looked. Everyone wanted to know about life in America. It was only as I heard myself answering their questions and telling them stories that I realized how much California had come to seem like home. Like any home, it wasn't a place I'd chosen freely. There were so many constraints that guided me to that particular place, so many ties that kept me there. But I'd learned to embrace it, and towards the end of my three-week trip, to my surprise, I even found that I missed it.

My sister did her best to understand this. To her, I seemed like a new version of Hana, like some kind of hybrid plant. Many things were the same, but so many other things were different. She was disappointed that I hadn't brought David with me. She longed to meet her nephew. When I told her the story of Brian's disappearance, she pressed her lips together and didn't respond. I'm sure one part of her had anticipated an outcome like this, but she never would have voiced such a feeling. And even though I kept many of the details from her, I'm sure she guessed more than I realized at the time. But the important thing for her was that I was safe, and secure, and happy. And for the first time in a long time, I was.

I arranged for everything I'd bought to be shipped back to San Francisco and boarded the plane at Seoul Airport with no one to wave me goodbye. If I'd known at the time that I wouldn't be back for more than a decade, would it have made any difference? My feeling that day was that of someone who has narrowly avoided a trap. I was euphoric, edgy, and shaken.

Back in San Francisco, I threw myself into my work. I spent days at the auction houses, talking to dealers, keeping an eye on my investments, learning what progressed quickly and what was harder to sell. There was so much adrenaline flowing through the enormous warehouse spaces that it sometimes felt like swimming as I moved from object to object, studying the detail of carved cabinets, running my hands over smooth black lacquer. I loved the guesswork, I loved the rush, and I loved the feeling of victory that went along with a profitable sale. The excitement of it pulled me up to the surface, away from the grief that still sometimes tugged at my ankles and threatened to pull me down. I felt I had finally kicked free.

Now that I felt stable enough to take the time to look around, there was one man in particular who stood out in the crowd. He came to the auction house one summer day carrying a small men's handbag and wearing a beautiful blue blazer. On those August days the warehouse was like a greenhouse, warm and steamy and teeming with life. None of the other men wore blazers or carried bags. It was the first time I'd seen him, so I assumed he was new, and probably not from California, where the standard uniform for men doing this sort of work at that time was tight bellbottom jeans and thin short-sleeved paisley shirts. At one point we stood next to each other and exchanged a brief glance, nothing more. In the excitement of selling a whole set of Japanese woodblock prints, I quickly forgot about him. Even when I got a call from a man with a clipped East Coast accent inquiring about a delicate Japanese cabinet I had for sale, I was unable to call his face to mind. All I could see was his blazer, and I wondered.

Sam came to my showroom on a bright Friday morning just as I was opening, running a cloth over the furniture and straightening a few of the prints on the walls. I recognized his blazer and his bag. I suppose he recognized me. His eyes fastened on mine for the briefest instant, then he held out a firm, smooth hand and told me he had phoned about the lacquer cabinet. He wanted it as an end table in his apartment, and he wanted it right away. He seemed like a man who was used to getting everything he wanted immediately. He was formal, even when he planted kisses in the air next to each of my cheeks. But as we wandered into a conversation beyond price and delivery details and on into the history of the Meiji period and other beautiful objects we'd each seen on our travels, he began to crack smiles and make dry, sly comments, and I found myself smiling back. I was intrigued.

He settled into a Thai elephant saddle chair, seemingly unperturbed by the hard wood and the carving that made the back of the chair difficult to lean against. The polished teak set off his short blond hair and blue shirt, and I could not stop looking at him. He seemed to take this attention in stride, as if it was nothing more than what he expected. We talked through the morning, in bits and snatches, and he sat patiently while I talked with other customers. When we ran out of things to say about the objects in my care, the conversation turned more personal, and he invited me to lunch. I learned that he was from New York, a hedge fund manager recently relocated to California after a big deal had left him with enough money to take some time off. He told me he liked the slower pace of life on the West Coast. He loved to sit on Torpedo Wharf and gaze out at the bay, to imagine the crisp blue sky behind the fog, the sleek sharks under the waves, the enormous tension in the cables holding the Golden Gate Bridge perilously over the water. I found myself wanting to confide in him, to tell him about my fear and fascination with the ocean, how the waves terrified me and drew me in at the same time. He was patient, quiet, a good listener. I left the meal feeling lighter.

The next day he came in the afternoon, in a beautiful terra cotta suit, and invited me to dinner. I said yes, thinking it was a casual affair, and was taken aback to be whisked away in his chauffeured car to the nicest restaurant I'd ever been in. Crystal chandeliers and glasses, linen tablecloths and napkins, and me in a summer dress and sandals. He ordered a bottle of wine and asked gently probing questions about my life. Where I was from. What I had studied. Whether I was married. I found myself pouring out the story, and he listened without betraying much emotion. He nodded often and seemed to accept everything, to take it all in without asking questions, and I found this strangely comforting. I told him about Brian, about Jim, about David. I told him about my childhood, about Seoul, and even about my paintings.

When I asked about him, he talked about art. He told me he collected Shunga, a particular form of Japanese erotic art, golden and delicate. We talked about Ukiyo-e, the art of the floating world, and its focus on pleasure, forgetting cares and worries. I pointed out that the homonym in Japanese, written with different characters but pronounced exactly the same, refers to the sorrowful world, the cycle of death and rebirth from which Buddhists seek release. He sat up straighter as I spoke, and fixed me with eyes that had frequently wandered around the room up until that point. From that moment, we were standing on different ground.

We didn't become a couple so much as we simply started spending every day together. He would arrive in the morning and sink into one of the many uncomfortable chairs in my showroom, telling me about some new object he'd acquired or about a trip he wanted to take. He was patient when I dealt with other customers. He liked to come with me to the auction floor, and several times he surprised me by making very expensive purchases. He preferred Japanese erotic art and intricate antique cabinets with dozens of drawers and secret compartments hidden away, drawers within drawers behind gorgeous locked doors.

He never pushed me to deepen our relationship romantically, and in time I came to feel I could rely on him. For more than a year, we talked, walked, ate, and just spent time together. I took my time examining him from different angles, like one of the objects I collected, evaluating its beauty and value. I found myself attracted to his introversion. His mind was extremely analytical and mathematical. He traded in facts, not feelings, and I liked the way our views of the world clashed. I found his perspective so alien as to be endlessly fascinating. We could talk for hours without agreeing on anything, but this deepened our separate understandings of the world we found ourselves in. His relentless drive to understand his life, to test his reality, drew me in completely. I came to love his reserve, his quiet self-containment. He presented a different kind of silence than my father, whose detachment was constantly shattered by angry emotional outbursts and violence. Sam was always carefully controlled. He never spoke without thinking first. I found safety and security in that.

He was also the polar opposite of Brian. Where Brian had been carried away by emotion, had spiraled out of control on waves of depression and anxiety, Sam had direction and purpose. Like Brian, he could discuss theories and philosophy, he could and did question society, but unlike Brian, he was never going to disappear into the woods. If he was slightly stiff, if he left many of his desires unspoken, I took this as proof that he would never drown in his own need, that he would never inadvertently make the kinds of demands Brian had made. Even as we grew to love each other, I knew he was holding back. But mostly I was happy to have found someone who seemed so different from all the men I had encountered in my life so far.

Sam infiltrated David's life, too. He started to look and act almost distressingly like a father figure. He brought thoughtful gifts, and David began to ask for him daily. I started to feel as though we were two lost souls who had finally found each other.

One Saturday morning, when Sam came to my showroom as usual, he had a postcard in his hand. He held it out to me without a word, and I took it from him and studied the ethereal view of a tangerine sun sinking into a violet ocean in a frame of feathery cypress trees and indigo lupine. I smiled and told him it was beautiful. When I reached out to hand it back, he took my hand and asked if I'd like to go there. I laughed, shrugging off the serious light in his eyes. Of course, I joked, anytime. He turned to the two people who were browsing in the shop and apologized, informed them that unfortunately we would have to close early today. I was too shocked to disagree, too entangled in that "we" to think clearly. He took me to his car outside, took me home to pack an overnight bag. I asked Jim to take care of David, told him I'd be back the next day. And Sam whisked me down the coast to the very spot where the photo had been taken. The balcony of a suite at the Post Ranch Inn.

But when I returned to Jim and David on Sunday evening, awash in the sense that I'd fallen into the floating world in the prints Sam surrounded himself with, Jim was stern with me. As soon as David was asleep, he called me into the living room and sat down across from me, his hands folded between his knees.

"I'd like to know more about this Sam."

My mind snagged on the word "this," as if Sam was only allegedly his name. I told him what I knew with the giddy feeling of the young girl I had never had the chance to be.

"Well, he's from New York. His father survived the Holocaust and came to America. Sam's a hedge fund manager. But I already told you that."

He stared across the coffee table with such a serious expression that I began to fidget.

"What else? He collects Japanese art. He's a good listener. And he makes me happy."

Jim listened with a sad smile on his face.

"Hana, I've seen you with Sam over the last few months. I know he makes you happy." Now it was Jim's turn to fidget. "But I've also watched him carefully. Especially his interactions with David. You know that's important to me." He lifted his chin like a boxer. "And I don't trust him."

I sat in shocked silence, my hands stilled in my lap.

"There's just something about him. Something missing, you know? Maybe you don't understand what I mean."

I was already shaking my head.

"Look, Hana. You know I care about you. About David. And there is just something I would want to see, some feeling in the person you choose to share your life with. And David's life too. But with Sam," he sighed. "I'm afraid for you."

My shock began to melt under the simmering heat of my anger.

"Some feeling? You don't think Sam has feelings?"

He held up both hands to calm me, but I was determined to speak. He talked over me.

"Hana, come on. A man who spends his professional life hiding things is not a good partner for someone as open and giving as you."

I clutched my hands between my knees, tried to control my anger. I spoke quietly.

"You don't think I'm capable of making my own choices, organizing my own life? Is that it? Or is it that you want me to stay here forever. With you."

I'd grown up in my father's ominous shadow, under the instructive care of monks and teachers, living quietly with my brother-in-law's restrictions during my student years. I'd left all that behind, only to be faced with Brian's oppressive needs and demands. I'd had love, but never freedom. Now I felt I'd found a balance of both. And for the first time, I saw Jim as another man trying to control my life. I saw his help, his investment, even the home he'd so generously shared with me and with David as another kind of trap. As I roiled and seethed internally, battered with this sudden wash of emotion, Jim set the bait.

"You should be doing something with your life. Something bigger. You could go back to school." I gaped at him. He leaned across the table to me. "I could help."

I found myself struggling not to laugh. It all seemed so ridiculous.

"And what would I study?"

"Psychotherapy."

"What? Why?"

"You have great insight. You should be using it for a larger cause. Helping people." He folded his hands between his knees. "Hana, you will never be happy if you let him make you just another piece of Asian art in his collection."

I didn't trust myself to speak. I stared at him. My mind flashed to my mother's face. Her predictions, her insights. So Jim envisioned me as a modern, urban shaman. Educated, well-dressed, but essentially just a less primitive version of my mother. And that was certainly not what I wanted to be.

"I could pay your tuition."

I stood up.

"Jim, no amount of money could ever convince me to do something I didn't want to do." I watched his face crumple. "And no matter what you think, my affection is not for sale."

I turned, went upstairs to my room, and quietly closed the door. Immediately I was swept away on a wave of tears that left me stranded on the floor, a grief much deeper than anger, or humiliation, much more than the strain Jim's words had put on our friendship. The things I wanted most, the things I'd missed out on in my life, had been love and family. Brian had been the only one who wanted me, and then he had abandoned me. Sam was different than Brian, different than my father. Steadfast, self-contained, solid. What I wanted more than anything was the kind of safety that came from a stable family, the warmth I wanted to give my son.

When Sam arrived at my showroom the next day, golden and glowing from our weekend together, I told him what Jim had said. I tried to make it a joke, a jealous man afraid of losing the strange little family we'd built together, but he didn't laugh, and I found myself fighting back more tears. He looked grave, but not surprised. Nothing ever seemed to surprise him. I wanted him to hold me, to squeeze the pain and the tears from my body, but in this public space, he simply put a hand on my arm and kissed my cheek.

And then he disappeared.

I spent the day in a daze, talking to customers, making deals, all the while wondering whether Sam would return. Whether what I'd said had so deeply offended his considerable pride that he'd decided he was better off without me. I played the scenario out in my head over and over, asking myself what I'd do if he never came back, convincing myself that I would be OK. That I had learned to stand on my own two feet, that I didn't need anyone to complete me. I knew it was the truth. Yet still I watched the door and waited.

As I was locking up the showroom he reappeared, one

hand in his pocket. In his matter-of-fact way, he said he had something to tell me. I steeled myself for the worst. That he'd gotten all he wanted from me. That the idea of taking on David as well as me was too much. That he couldn't see a future for us. And then he held out a small box.

Inside was a delicate platinum band I recognized from one of the other showrooms in the warehouse. We had admired it together months ago. He told me he wanted to marry me. He didn't ask, didn't get down on one knee, he simply said he loved me and he thought we should get married. My mind flashed to Brian and his Sears catalogue of gaudy diamond rings, and I had to laugh. But reality quickly swept in to sober me up.

"Sam, I love you. But you know my story." My breath rattled in my throat. "I'm already married."

It was true. Brian had disappeared, but divorcing him in absentia would take a herculean effort of lawyers and private investigators. I would have to contact his family. His former employers. His landlords. And I could not face that.

"It takes seven years." Jim had told me this. I had trouble speaking the rest of the sentence aloud. "It takes seven years for a missing person to be declared dead."

Sam took the ring out of the box, slipped it onto my finger.

"I can wait."

He gave me his sly smile. And I said yes.

In retrospect, the Post Ranch Inn should have been a clue. But I don't think I realized the extent of Sam's wealth until he offered to buy David and I a house.

After Sam and I decided to marry, I knew I could not continue living with Jim. We'd apologized to each other, and I wanted to forgive him, but we couldn't easily put a conversation like that behind us. I'd already begun looking at apartments, small two-bedroom places on the outskirts of the city. But even these were expensive. I wanted a place with good light and room to paint, a place with a small yard, or at least with a park nearby where David could play. But the more I looked, the more it became clear that I had a better chance of finding buried treasure in Golden Gate Park than finding the perfect apartment.

I poured out my frustration to Sam one night while I cooked dinner at his apartment. He loved French food, and I'd begun experimenting with Julia Child's recipes. I told him about that afternoon's showing as I tenderized the meat.

"The whole place smelled like mold and rot." I thwacked a piece of beef. "And the neighbors upstairs? You could hear every step right through the ceiling."

Sam twirled the stem of his wineglass, studied me as I swiveled from the sink to the kitchen island to the stove and back again.

"Why don't you let me buy us a house?"

The spoon in my hand clattered into his stainless steel sink. It was the way he suggested it so casually, like he was picking up the check for dinner. As though it was completely natural to buy a house with a yard for your fiancée's child to play in.

"But—" I started the sentence before I knew how to finish it.

"But what? We can't get married yet, but we could live together. Why not? Why should we have to wait for a piece of paper before we start our life as a family?"

The astronomical San Francisco real estate prices didn't seem to enter into his equation. I knew he had made enough money in New York to take time out and live a good life in California, but it hadn't occurred to me to try to estimate what kind of sum that might take. I turned to where David sat on the tile floor, playing an overturned pot like a drum. I knew what would be best for him.

As time went on, more hints seeped out, one little clue at a time. I should have guessed that a man in his early thirties who knew so much about Asian antiques and was already taking time off from a job he'd only had for a few years must have had a significant financial cushion to fall back on. At the time, I was too happy to think much about it. But slowly I learned.

I learned that his mother had never worked. She had gone straight from her father's house into a marriage that was not so different in its origins from the arranged marriages I'd grown up with in Korea. Although it was different in every other way. I learned that his father and his grandfather had both been bankers. That he'd been bred to his profession and never questioned it. That his father's career had been interrupted by the Second World War, that he had survived the Holocaust and started over in New York with nothing. That he was a self-made man. I learned that Sam had spent time as a child on Martha's Vineyard with famous writers, actors, and artists. I learned that his sister had been given a house in the Vermont countryside as a wedding present. Sam wondered aloud which piece of family property we might receive when we married. From these hints, I learned what it meant to be a member of New York's upper crust. And I began to wonder what I'd gotten myself into.

Still, I thought we would be different. I thought Sam loved my work and understood why I did it. I thought he admired the fact that I had taken my life into my own hands, that I'd survived. That he'd fallen in love with that version of me. I had left Korea wanting to look up to Brian, determined to accept him for who he was, but almost immediately I'd had to take responsibility for him, for a baby, and finally for myself. Having watched Brian deteriorate, I did not want to rely on another man. Not Jim, not Sam. I'd had enough of taking care. I wanted to take control. I wanted to give my son all the love I'd missed out on. And I had succeeded. I'd developed the power and confidence to survive on my own. I was modestly financially independent. I went into my relationship with Sam thinking we were equal partners, and assuming it would continue that way.

I was wrong, of course. The house he bought for us was only the first of many boxes he kept me in. But hindsight is perfectly clear, while our vision of the present is cloudy. And at that time, there was no way I could have predicted what the next three decades would bring.

Chapter 5:
Ennui

Where have
all our dreams gone?

Inevitable ennui,
overexposed negatives.

Emotions exasperate,
the spirit defaults to boredom.

Perhaps
it's all seam(less)ly connected.

Seduced by
unavoidable circumstances,
visited by an apprehension –

Fatigue,
coming, then going,
with no meaningful anticipation.

Sam cannot understand people who hold themselves back. Who curb their desires, their urges, their abilities. To what end? He can keep secrets, so there's no need for such weakness. And no excuse.

He knows how it is. He marries Hana because he loves her. Because it seems like the right time, the right thing to do. Because he knows he'll never do better. Because it's another box in his life that needs to be filled. Because he thinks he can have it all.

Maybe he doesn't know how it is.

Loyalty is an important quality. It doesn't have to be tempered with empathy to be effective. Empathy is over-rated. There are scientific studies to prove it. Empathy leads nowhere. Compassion is another weakness.

But that's not what his wife thinks.

He was a philanderer long before Hana. Long before San Francisco. It has something to do with putting people in boxes. Compartments. The lovely little individual drawers that make up a delicate Japanese lacquer cabinet. How smoothly they open and close. Even after centuries.

He loves Hana. He loves anything Asian. He has always been a professional collector. Of art, antiques, furniture, women. A compulsive straightener, obsessed with order, cleanliness, and control.

If his wife had asked him outright, he might have admitted it. That monogamy was not for him, that marital fidelity was not something he felt the need to strive for. Balance is the thing. And a capacity for keeping secrets. Love doesn't enter into it. Love was never the problem.

He did his best. No one can ask for more than that.

It began with the New York apartment. After the wedding, he went back to work. After years of happy relaxation, of love and care, of focusing on his new role as a husband

and father. He liked the version of himself he glimpsed in Hana and David's eyes. But his office and his clients were in New York. Hana's work and David's school were in San Francisco. He commuted. Just once a month, at first. He bought a new apartment. His own place. And he cultivated opportunity. But for years, nothing happened. He always called home to tell his wife he loved her. He never missed a night. And he never didn't mean it.

It was her generous empathy he loved first. That down-to-earth quality impressed him. It was not threatening in his wife, that quality he had purged as a weakness in himself. She was trusting, open. And her mind made him sit up straight, look her in the eye. She was different than the women he'd collected by the handful during those first successful years in New York. He felt genuine love. Respect. He thought that would be enough.

Picture Hana in her twenties. Engaging, attentive, insightful. A high achiever, yet unconditionally support-ive, extravagantly generous. That was one reason for the attraction. And it was a powerful attraction. She filled in his gaps. They fit together like a puzzle cabinet. In the beginning, they were wonderful, these differences. He needed her at his side. Separate but equal. Then he wanted her for his own. He valued her as he would an antique woodblock print. Rare. Unique. Irreplaceable. Years later, when she finally escaped from her embellished box, when she demanded air to breathe, he was surprised. And also relieved.

Hana was his choice. His lover and his healer. He

had money, but she had an internal wealth he was starved for. Her introspection and insight were his stabilizers. At first. But his desire grew like mold in an unaired room. A live thing that breathed and could not be contained, only killed or set free.

Until he met Hana, he'd had regular contact with escorts, but that had stopped after they moved in together. He loved her, and he loved David. He loved the part of himself he saw playing the role of a good husband, a good father. Their first ten years together were very happy. He worked hard at creating a little tableau he could point to. Look, how happy we are together.

When Sam returned to New York, David was just starting first grade, and he and Hana wanted to have another child. But she was having trouble conceiving. She wanted to accompany him to Manhattan, to keep their family together, to try to grow in a new place. But he wanted his own space. He encouraged her to stay in San Francisco, with David's school, her job, her friends. Reluctantly, she agreed. Eventually, she took a part-time job as a chef in a little French restaurant. Sam was enthusiastic about her expanding expertise in French cooking, but jealous of her time and her care.

As time went on and his wife flourished, Sam resented her growing independence. He needed to be able to rely on Hana to stay in the compartment of home and family. After their daughter Mia was born, he insisted that Hana should give up her job and stay home with the baby. He was delighted with her, this perfect little creature. The little girl became another thing to slip into the family drawer. Her needs and wants were met by others. Sam was Daddy for a few moments on weekends. Those moments felt great, so long as they were kept carefully within their limits. He wanted to control Hana, his children. To control how they remembered him, their visions of him in the present.

But he needed more than a family. A wife and children by themselves were not sufficient. He cared about them deeply, but they inhabited one compartment of his life. There were others. He had no intention of leaving his family. Not ever. But he felt he was entitled to more. To a private life. He worked hard. He was stressed. He needed to unwind. And as long as no one found out, then no one could get hurt. No harm done.

He picked up his old habits after he returned to New York. He started spending nearly every week in the city, returning to San Francisco only twice a month. He began searching out the escort agencies he'd used before his marriage. He could find no other way to express what had to be released. He didn't have the capacity to hold himself back. And he didn't like the husband he became. Coldness seeped in, an old cruelty he recognized but could not escape.

He punished Hana for putting up with him. She accepted his emotional limitations. Maybe it was the years of childhood abuse that had nearly drowned her. She was tranquil, generous, almost pathologically suited to enabling him. Repressed, depressed, he slipped into the old dark well. He told her he needed novelty. He felt as if he was looking at her through a sheet of clear ice. He couldn't touch her. And she shivered under his chill. She began to tiptoe around him, as if she were afraid. He liked this. But not in his wife.

At first, he tried to hoist himself back into the light by intensifying his devotion to his favorite collections. The darker his mood, the more extravagant the object. Cases of extraordinary wine. Bespoke golf clubs. Rare opera recordings. When the recordings no longer satisfied, he traveled the world to witness performances firsthand, often taking Hana with him. But none of these obsessions offered the warmth he needed to melt the ice. Women solved that problem.

Concubines, he called them. He thought of himself as a sultan. A collector of women, a fantasy based on the grandeur of the ancient Alhambra Palace in Spain.

He considered himself a feminist. All for equal treatment, equal opportunity. He assumed his wife had her own affairs. That she kept them in a dark drawer, as he did. As long as her love remained a reliable link, as long as it always pulled her back, he didn't mind. He believed in reciprocity.

What he could not understand was her resistance to his logical solution. All her talk of soul, of faithfulness. For him, loyalty was not a sexual question. And a life built together over decades was not something he would ever throw away for sex. He came up with other solutions. When she complained of loneliness, he encouraged her to take a lover. He suggested an open relationship, with carefully hewn tracks for the little drawers to follow, locks and keys to use when things needed to be kept hidden away. It was simple logic. It made sense. He didn't understand the alternative.

Betrayal was not a word Sam would apply to what he did. He always saw himself as committed. He kept Hana, and kept her in the dark. For her own good. And it was a luxurious cabinet, too. Even the Japanese art on the walls was stylish in all its exquisite, pornographic detail.

Privacy was another of Sam's absolutes. In his line of work, it was a necessity. His professional specialty was spiriting away, managing risk, keeping complicated transactions under lock and key. That was how he was raised. His cell phone, his laptop, his office, all off-limits. For good reason. Many good reasons.

He did try. No one can accuse him of not making the effort. But the center just didn't hold.

He'd learned early on that transactions are best when they are not emotional. He always had trouble bonding. Even when it came to sex. Escort agencies were the simplest solution. No strings. He could take a woman to dinner, expect everyone in the restaurant to notice her. He could take her to his apartment, and when it was all over she would get up and leave. He knew his own weaknesses. He was always quite self-aware. But he had the wherewithal to indulge himself and the cast of mind to tease out the different strands of his life and keep them separate. Sam valued that kind of cold courtesy. He thought of this as strength, a stroke of good luck.

Plus it was reciprocal. The women he was with wanted money, and they got it. Maybe also some other, more nebulous form of validation, but that was not his concern. Money kept things clean. Money for a service. Money to give orders and have them obeyed. Money to keep secrets. Any business transaction is prostitution. Any service provided. It's not just the oldest profession, it's the only profession.

And it's not as if he's the only one.

The world he grew up in was full of compartments. He was raised to believe that problems are something to be kept, like secrets. He watched his father hold his past close to his chest, where no one else could see. He never spoke of it. Not of the horrors of the war, not of the life he'd lived before the camps. Sam wouldn't have known at all if his mother hadn't told him.

His mother and father loved each other fiercely, possessively, with the kind of devotion that comes from the knowledge that everything can be swept away in a moment. Sam grew up secure in that love. He learned French, his mother's language, and German, his father's. He spoke to them each in their different idioms. They created separate worlds for him, neat compartments for different types of devotion.

His boyhood home had large rooms with cathedral ceilings and waterfall silk curtains. His mother's rooms. His father's. His sister's. Spaces that were appropriate for children, and spaces that were not. Separate spaces that never met. Entire worlds contained in heavy oak and white plaster and paintings from another century. Everyone observed the boundaries, the formality. Emotion was for private spaces. So Sam learned to keep his anger on ice. The compact lacquered spaces of Asian art, when he encountered them, appealed to him because they were manageable.

His mother would smile gently, silently at him across the polished dining table. She taught him how to use his knife and fork, how to keep from scraping them against the plate, how to drink, how to wipe his lips. Never to talk with food in his mouth. Never to touch a plate or a bowl once it had been set down. Never to drag chairs across the floor. Meals should be silent except for single words uttered quietly, between bites.

His father never told stories. But he passed on his trauma in other ways, things too subtle to be firmly grasped. Things a small boy absorbs like roots absorb water. Sam went to the best private schools, where he was buffered, sheltered from the jostle of the Manhattan streets. He did not play sports, because his parents worried about injury. He did not go on school trips or spend weekends away from home. His parents needed to control his environment. They needed him to be safe.

Sam's demon was anxiety. Paranoia. His mother's

therapist prescribed lithium for his panic attacks. The ups and downs of his mental maze were easier to cut off than to explore. He held the pads of his fingers over matches, filled glasses to the brim, pushed priceless glass art objects to the very edge of shelves, until they teetered. And when the predictable came to pass – a burn, a cascade, a shatter – he felt an enormous sense of relief. He smiled.

As he grew, he became vehemently territorial. Disappearing into his dark room in a cold sweat, drowning in another panic attack, he always locked the door behind him. He never talked about his struggles over those silent dinners. If there were tears, they were his alone.

In the dark, he discovered the laser focus that would guide him through life. He developed a work ethic. In middle school, he completed every task asked of him, but increasingly avoided group activities. He cultivated a reputation as a shy, reclusive boy. A sensitive soul. His academic record was faultless. Every top mark he earned gave him a euphoric high to rival the lithium. He learned the pleasure of strict control.

His first sexual experience was two-dimensional. He was young, no more than thirteen, when Japanese woodblock prints at a special exhibition at the Metropolitan Museum of Art aroused him for the first time. He became obsessed with Ukiyo-e. He aspired to that floating world, to its beauty, its removal from reality, and its gilded sex. He fantasized about delicate Asian women. He bought his first print with the money he inherited when he turned eighteen, from the trust fund his mother's parents had set up before the war. At twenty, he traveled to Tokyo to learn more, to buy more. He encountered Chunga for the first time, erotic woodblock prints that focused on feminine curves, close-ups of the intricate details of nipples or pubic hair, all in a mélange of colors imprinted on rice paper. He arranged a private tour of a collection, and bought them all. His parents were impressed.

The prints were intended as fantasy, snapshots of life lifted out of the mundane world, no more real than a seventeenth-century still life depicting a dead rabbit and a bowl of fruit in layers of oil and shadow. He was aroused as much by possessing the collection as by the images themselves. When he landed his first big bonus, he took a collecting trip to Asia. Eventually his interest took him to the auctions in San Francisco. Where he met Hana. She understood his fascination as an artistic sensibility. She helped him collect. She bought prints for him as presents. He convinced himself that this made her complicit in the rest of his activities, too.

For Sam, these were easy leaps – from collecting academic awards and professional success to collecting art and music to collecting women. Emotional intimacy was not something he'd seen modelled in his family, and certainly not something he thought he wanted. The time between penetration and ejaculation was as intimate as he got. For him, bonding was a solely sexual act.

In the professional circles in which he moved, affairs were the norm. Monogamy was derided as unsophisticated, artificial. These unrealistic, puritanical American ideals of romance and fidelity were the real problem. If only he could have been honest with Hana from the beginning. Had she known about the compartments, maybe she could have accepted them. It was the shock of discovered deception that opened the door to all their misery. Knowing and choosing to look the other way would have been something else. But he believed this guilt was artificial. It was not natural. It was not helpful. He refused to accept it. Desires are nothing to feel guilt over. Sex and desire are highly individual. They are not naturally suited to relationships. They shouldn't be public issues.

Sex is gratification and release. Sex is sex, and relationship is relationship. More sex is better. It's healthy. It's a stress release. Like smoking. Or drinking. Everybody has their self-medication.

Back in New York, less than a year after his wedding, he starts with a secretary. Young, slinky, clichéd. For both of them, it's just a bit of fun. When he gets a promotion, she stays behind to work for his successor, and he takes on a new role with two new assistants. Things fizzle. But after that first dalliance he's hyperaware, immediately noticing anyone in the office who looks at him twice. There are opportunities everywhere. But when one of those chances develops feelings and begins making demands, he switches to paid sex. Transactional sex. It's more fun, less risk. A win–win. Paying for it means he can still claim to love his wife, and even tell all the other women so. They have to admire him even as they service him. He doesn't have to reciprocate. It's safe. Controlled. He pays for deception, and he's complicit in it.

The inheritance he comes into after his parents die makes things worse. Money exacerbates the problem, though it's not the cause. His pleasure is deep, sharp, like a needle prick. Like an inoculation. The next dose always has to be stronger. The updraft is intoxicating. Investing in his hobbies means investing in the enhancement required to enjoy them. Whether that's good stereo equipment for his opera recordings, a well-built cellar for his wine, or performance drugs for his women.

He imagines himself as an actor on a stage. He plays a different part for each one of his audiences. He refuses to accept the opinions of critics. He knows that feeling just before the curtain goes up, when he can hear his audience murmuring, the odd burst of laughter like gunfire. When the lights dim and, for a second, it's just him and a thousand blank stares. Maybe he's an exhibitionist after all. There's always somebody watching. That's euphoria. The way the maître-d recognizes him, gives him the best table. The way the owner of the restaurant comes over with wine selected especially for him. The way other diners stare.

He likes exhibitionists. People who lose control, so he can prove his. Yet he fantasizes about being caught. The imagined arousal of asserting his control over that narrative, too. It turns him on.

He has understanding colleagues. Others who close ranks with him to protect their own indiscretions. An unspoken agreement. He has few friends. He has power. He knows many men in his position sleep with secretaries, the wives of colleagues and friends, women they pick up on dating sites. He never worries about watching his back. He abhors transparency. Privacy is essential to any sort of meaningful existence. The keeping of secrets, his own and others.

In New York one chill winter evening, he's enjoying a fine meal in one of his favorite restaurants. He's hired a girl who sits pressed against him on the rounded leather bench seat, one hand on his thigh, squeezing. Playing with fire. A shadow falls over the table and he looks up, his grin fading. It's Carol, one of Hana's friends from the board of the San Francisco Opera. She doesn't greet him. She eyes the girl.

"Hana has that exact same necklace."

Before he can respond, she crosses the room to where her party has just been seated. He keeps an eye on her. Later, when she gets up to go to the restroom, he follows.

"Carol," he smiles. "How are you?"

She doesn't return the gesture.

"I can guess what this must look like." He leans his weight onto his back foot. "That woman? She's this crazy colleague of mine. She's been trying to get me to go out to dinner with her for months. I finally gave in."

Carol tilts her head up at him. Sam rushes on.

"She's probably trying to seduce me or something." He aims for a nonchalant chuckle. "But she's young. Obviously just chasing a promotion."

Carol slices her hand through the air to cut him off.

"Look, Sam." She gives him a look full of pity. "Don't worry. It's not my place to tell Hana anything."

He holds himself rigid, tries not to let the relief show on his face.

"A piece of advice? You should think twice. About what you really want."

The door to the bathroom closes behind her, and he returns to his table, shaking his head. He doesn't see why he should have to choose. It's all what he wants.

He grows increasingly brazen. Something in him needs the thrill. He watches women strip for him on webcams while his wife makes dinner in the next room. Strange lingerie surfaces in his luggage when he returns to San Francisco on weekends. He checks and responds to text messages while he sits across from Hana in their living room. Sometimes he looks up to find her eyes on his face, but she never asks who's on the other end of the line. It wouldn't have mattered if she had.

He has a problem, it's true. He's too astute not to know that. But that doesn't have to mean accepting blame. He's not at fault. He was never at fault. He can feed his ego, or fear it, but he can't fight it. Everyone knows how good intentions can be steamrolled by strong desire.

He loves the story of Casanova, except for the ending.

Casanova gave up too early. A cozy retirement at a library in Bohemia. Acquiescing to the softness of his body, the fatigue in his soul. He didn't see the point in continuing. The game had lost its charm. God forbid that should ever happen to Sam.

In his old age, Casanova craves justification. He wants to explain. He is a victim of his senses. A heroic sufferer. He went astray. But Sam knows he knew. He knew the destruction he waged, the consequences of his entrapment. At least Sam is not so disingenuous as to cry *mea culpa* and beg forgiveness. Many people walk blindly through life, unaware of the pain they cause. At least he is not guilty of that.

Out of all of them, Stella was his mistake. He let that get out of hand. She expected too much. And she had too much evidence.

Stella was a collectible. Passed on by a colleague when his wife discovered their affair. Sam was intrigued by the handover. The consignment of a precious object. He first met her on one of his trips to New York. Tragic, pouty lips, voluptuous curves. He warmed to her immediately. She was a university student at the time, interested in both the money and the adventure. She was from Montreal and spoke beautiful French, like his mother. She'd spent time in Paris as a girl. She felt so familiar. It was a heady sense of homecoming. She was charming and feisty, not limp like some of the escorts he'd hired, shouting out her orgasms to prove something she thought she'd deduced that he needed. Stella seemed to know instinctively how to fulfill his fantasies. And the high he got from conquering her rivalled anything he'd ever gotten from psychotropic drugs.

He managed to see her nearly every week. His weekends in California grew shorter and narrower. But when she told him she'd fallen in love with him, it came as a surprise. He'd been clear that emotional involvement was not on the table. A simple exchange of sex for money. Only the present moment to enjoy. She insisted he could trust her. As if trust were ever the issue.

That was the moment. He should have run then. He should have applied the same rule he'd used with all the others. But it was Stella. He was sure Stella was different. He wanted to make that exception. He convinced himself she was in love with love, that he was simply the nearest target. It wasn't really about him at all. She talked about the future. He sent her more money.

That's when the photos began. He'd always been careful there, too. No evidence. No trace. But she brought her own camera, and there were two other women in bed with him, and it was impossible to say no without ruining the moment. Instant gratification trumped caution. In the end, that trickling loss of control was his undoing.

She wrote the first letter later that week. An email. About how much she enjoyed watching him with other women. She wanted to hear more of his fantasies. He offered to pay her for more photos. He wanted to discover her threshold. How long it would take before she stopped talking about love and started making demands. But he never got the opportunity. He held out for humiliation, reached for the control that would let him make her small. But she always asked for more.

It never occurred to Sam that he was the one in the trap. A trail of traded fantasy weaving its way through electronic space. They built up trust, each deceiving the other. Motivations are slippery things. Sam knew that, in theory.

In the end, her motivation, the only one Sam could admit to himself, turned out to be one he understood. Money. He'd held it out, taken it away, and she wanted it back doubled. Money bought what he wanted. It also squelched him in its web. He'd always feared retaliation once a woman figured out what more she could demand in return for her silence. So he relied on withholding, self-protection, knowing the moment to retreat. With Stella, he thought he'd found mutual loyalty. He'd let his guard down.

Afterwards, when it was all over, he confronted her.

"You realize you'll never have me all to yourself, right?" He kept his voice tight, controlled, balled up in the back of his throat. "That's not how this is going to go."

She pointed her chin at him. "Is that really what you think I care about?" She scoffed. "I don't. I don't care about you."

His exasperation got the better of him. He flung his hands into the air. "Then what?"

"Deception," she hissed. "Deception is the reason you deserved this. All of this." She circled her hands in the air. "At least I never lied. Not to you, not to anybody."

Dragging the truth out into the light, kicking and screaming. That was the upper hand.

She jabbed the air between them with a furious finger. "You should have known!"

He staggered. Not under the weight of her hate, but under the blow of betrayal. Loyalty was the least he could expect, and he had expected it of her.

It was the last time they ever spoke.

After Mia was born, Sam decided they needed more space. He found a plot of land overlooking the sea, north of the city. He wanted to help Hana build her dream home. A house in the hills, a swimming pool, beautiful gardens. He and Hana had travelled to Spain, to Granada, and seen the Alhambra. They'd both fallen in love with the space and the light, and their new home was modelled on its beautiful Moorish architecture, with black river stones in the walls and the fireplaces. Every room had a private entrance and a garden. Sam reconstructed the Concubine Garden, down to the last detail. A long rectangular pool bordered by slabs of slate and trimmed myrtle hedges, backed by three hundred red roses. His wife accepted this pretty detail without ever asking why. The house was big. It had its own compartments. There were rooms for family, rooms for children, a suite for Sam and Hana, and a caretaker's cottage in anticipation of their old age. There was a studio for Hana, and a private office for him alone.

Hana wanted balance, harmony, transparency. Sam insisted on privacy. She gave it to him without protecting it for herself. Lost and regained his respect as a result. Emotional intimacy. The core of a good relationship. The rotten, moth-eaten core. He'd always preferred withdrawal. His own internal world, filled with fantasy, happily detached.

The new house had to be kept spotless. Sam would come home from the airport on Friday evenings, sweep his fingers over the books on the shelves, check the back of the toilet for curls of hair, look behind cabinets for cobwebs. He poked fun at the way his father's obsessions had resurfaced in his own life. Order. Control. But his wife never laughed.

The first time, she'd called him from the airport. Frantic, afraid he was ill, or missing. He'd been in bed with Stella all weekend and had neglected his usual calls home. When his wife finally reached him, he accused her of invading his privacy. She was tearful, angry. He flew home, and confessed. Said it was just this one time. Said he needed help. And he believed that. He offered to see a therapist, to go on medication. She agreed to try, to wait and see. When she noted his waning libido, he blamed the medication.

Cold kills. And Sam knew how to deploy frigidity as a weapon. He didn't touch Hana for years at a time. He told her it wasn't about her. She believed him. She always used to believe him. He grew silent, turned inward. He asked whether she would mind lending him to another woman for the night. She thought it was a joke, but she didn't laugh. She deflated. She grew thinner. She said not knowing was the best medicine. For once, they agreed.

She stayed for the sake of the children, of the family she'd worked so hard to build. She filled and refilled the drawer of love and attachment. But the drawer of desire was a different story. Sam kept filling it, but each time he returned to open it, it was empty, clamoring to be filled up again. He couldn't keep his balance. He couldn't tell his wife what he needed. What he wanted was beyond any words that could be spoken within the walls he'd constructed. Fantasy. Dominance. Novelty. He thought of himself as a sexual entrepreneur. His only pleasure was in starting things he didn't have the patience to finish.

Thirty years is a long time. Too long to be exciting. Too long to disregard. Too long to change. Sam felt he could work harder at being a good husband and father. And he would. If only Hana would allow him to wander.

When the skin is cut, both sides of the wound grow towards each other. They reach out for each other. And in healing, they meet. But the result is never the same as before the cut. It may be stronger. It may even be beautiful, in its way. But it is not the same as wholeness. Her flaws are not kin to his. He will never understand her.

It's a sunny autumn afternoon, a garden full of late-summer roses just past their bloom and starting to droop, petals falling. The scent is overwhelming. Sam circulates among the guests, glass of wine in hand, sipping, not really drinking. They're taking in the fountains, the views of the city, the bay between. A fundraiser for the opera house, a successful evening of music, wine, and food Hana made herself. Pledges are rolling in. Hana is happy. Her mouth, as ever, is a calm flat line, but her deep eyes glow with the low golden light of the setting sun. It's a moment of contentment. He smiles for her.

As the last guests are leaving, cars pulling away up the circular drive in front of the house, she disappears. Sam refills his glass and moves to the deck, watching the light change over the water, waiting for her to come. She always comes to him. But as the sun fades into a tangerine ball on the horizon and finally slips beneath the blanket of waves, a chill settles down for the night. She is not by his side. He goes in search of her, finds her sitting on the sofa with her laptop, hands resting on the serge at her sides, lips drooping a little.

"Tired?" He moves to her side, settles next to her to see what she's looking at. It's him, on the screen. On a bed with two women. Naked. Hana stares, unblinking. Sam's anger rises, but he pushes it down. Who? he thinks first. Then, "What's this?" he asks aloud, hating the stupid drone of his own voice.

It's not the only photo. In a matter of minutes, Hana has seen a cross-section of his secret life. As if the back of the cabinet had been cut away, and she could see into all the drawers at once. Photos. Graphic emails. And a request for money to keep it all quiet.

Sam hadn't considered this possibility. One part of him has to admire it. He never thought Stella had it in her. Almost immediately a wave of revulsion overtakes admiration. He hadn't protected himself adequately. Hadn't foreseen this. How could he have let things get so out of hand?

He knew Stella was angry. He was nearing retirement. There would be no more weekly business trips to New York. No reason to keep paying her the monthly fee she'd become accustomed to. He'd assumed she'd find other clients. When he explained, she'd seemed understanding. And he'd never expected anyone to be able to penetrate the multi-million dollar walls of his wife's compartment. He'd underestimated Stella.

His mind races ahead to wonder how much Hana has seen, how much she suspected already. How prepared she might have been. Maybe not exactly for this, but for something.

His wife sits on the sofa, laptop loose on her knees, forgotten. He tries to put his arms around her. She's rigid. There are no tears. He expects to melt her icy anger with his embrace, the first in a long time. But he's underestimated her, too. She wants to know how long. He tells her the truth. Always. He tells her it's nothing to do with her.

That's also the truth, but she can't hear it. She proclaims him a professional philanderer. She shouts him out of the room. When he reaches the door, she gathers herself, tells him calmly, quietly, to leave the house, then her life.

He feels no guilt. When she confronts him, he feels shame. But not guilt. Never.

He resists the divorce, ignores her lawyer's request for documents. His wife says he of all people should understand the need for self-preservation. He hadn't realized she saw him so clearly. The loss confounds him. Proof of his lack of control, even self-control. His panic attacks return. When he goes home to collect his clothes, he notices Hana's bare ring finger, the wedding band still visible in the paler skin where the ring had rested for three decades. Something reaches up and nooses his neck, and he finds he cannot breathe. He has the feeling of having lost something valuable, as if one of his works of art had been stolen. Or had liberated itself.

Divorce is frightening. Continuing the marriage is terrifying. The pressure is too great either way, from every side. There is the danger of ending up as before, detached and drifting. That drawer will always need to be filled, even though no one can manage it. Not even him.

He could forgive his wife the same indiscretions. He thinks that makes him better. More highly evolved. More realistic. More independent. He sees her need for him as a flaw. He has a mathematical mind. The equation of his life needs to involve both his wife and his escapades, both his family and his fantasies. Each of his collections, nicely catalogued, kept studiously apart. Surely Hana should be able to see that. He cannot exist without his affairs. She will have to exist with them. A call for change is not something he can accept.

In that final scene, when she ordered him out of the house, the first thing he did was dial the escort agency. Two girls, dressed for dinner, within the hour. He couldn't give it up. Even for something he wanted so badly. Yet what hurt most was relinquishing control.

The morning after, he is alone in the hotel room. The girls left hours ago. He hoists himself through his hangover and into the bathroom. He avoids his own eyes in the mirror. He's good at beginnings. Not good at endings.

His colleagues universally express how sorry they are to hear about the divorce. Like hell they are, he thinks. They can barely contain their glee as they watch his carefully constructed exterior crumble. He smells something coming from one of his cabinets. Something rotten. Mold, perhaps. Or spoiled food. What else it could be does not bear thinking about. He wonders if other people can smell it on him.

Hana is the only judge he will admit. Because she knows him. Because she is merciful. Because no one else has earned the right. He and his wife each alone, suffering together.

Sam hasn't spoken to Hana for years. She's the one who wants it that way. He tells himself he doesn't need her. He doesn't need.

The revelation, as Stella referred to it, had the strangest effect on Sam. He bowed out. When his colleagues cooled their contact, when his friends cut ties altogether, when his sister and her family took several large steps back and left him standing on the ledge alone, he jumped. His pride didn't buoy him up. It didn't push him to insist. No one understood his inability to step back from the fire. Least of all Sam.

So he lets them talk. Everyone who says he threw stones at the perfect glass house. That's just envy. Or that he hasn't even demonstrated remorse. That's their own guilt talking. That they never really knew him, or that they knew it all along. That's fear. They worry for Hana. But Hana will be fine. That's one thing Sam knows for sure.

Every piece of antique furniture has cracks. His delicate Meiji cabinets, as well preserved as they are, have wrinkles in the lacquer, splits in the wood, slivers in the paint. Lives are the same way. Live long enough, look close enough, and there they are. Most people only see those cracks in those they're closest to. But when someone shines a spotlight on those fine details, like overhead lighting and spiderweb wrinkles, it's too intimate, too horrific.

Years have passed. Not a day goes by that he doesn't think of Hana, of David, of Mia, and regret. But he hasn't reformed. He still can't seem to help himself.

He's stopped answering the phone. It's too much work. When loneliness hits, there are sex clubs, escort services. Ways to fill himself up by filling someone else. We are all perverse. The only difference is that Sam has publicly admitted it.

He remembers soft summer evenings at the Glyndebourne Opera Festival, black-tie picnics and high golden sunlight, champagne and drifting laughter. It was impossible to be unhappy then.

He's back on Martha's Vineyard, in the old family summer cottage. Another place of ghosts and dust. This time he's there as a hermit. But perhaps hermitage is a natural end for someone who can't sustain intimacy. When all the contacts are worn out and only the inner wiring is left.

The house is gone, sold with all its contents trapped inside. The golf clubs are gone. The wine is gone. The collection of Asian art remains. Crammed into this five-room house, with its wooden floors and mold crawling down from the rafters. With its dusty green velvet curtains sweeping the floor. Every inch of wall space reflects some Japanese artist's idea of the pornographic attractions of the floating world. Pushed back against the walls, standing at the ends of sofas, in place of cupboards in the kitchen, are the ancient lacquer cabinets handed down by samurai. Sam is surrounded by ancient strangers who understand. Order, distance. There are worse things.

The bedroom is the only place free of sex. Free of cabinets. Devoid even of curtains. The only ornament, besides the antique four-poster bed with its striped navy sheets, is a painting of Hana. A self-portrait in the style of Modigliani. Sam still wakes up to her every morning.

On their last anniversary, he opened a bottle of the same wine he'd bought her on their honeymoon in the south of France. The first wine she'd tasted and truly liked. Chateau Haut-Brion. He rolled it around on his tongue, eager for every last detail, wanting to feel again the specific qualities she'd loved. And he thought of the quantity of love she'd wasted on him.

He is truly pained to have caused pain. To the one person who should have been spared. Which was the reason for the compartments in the first place. The excitement was too much to resist. The pleasure was fleeting, unsustainable, exhausting, never exhaustive. Running out like water from a sieve. Some part of him knew this would happen. The drawer leaked. Could any love have shored it up? He'll never know. But he risked it nonetheless.

It was never sadism. He never wanted to hurt her. He wanted to keep his secrets. The contents of those cabinets made him less depressed, less withholding, less difficult to live with. He thought this would make him better within the confines of himself as husband and father. But it didn't work out that way.

It was never her shortcomings. His wife. Blaming her would be dishonest. An untruth. It has always been about himself. Blame does not figure.

He longs for truth. That's the limited good he can still strive for. He never wants to hurt her again. But more than that, most of all, he doesn't want to hurt himself. Giving her up hurt. Giving up his parallel lives would have hurt just as much. Truth is the most he can hope for. That and the strength not to repeat past mistakes.

Now, in this overcrowded room, all he can think, over and over again, is that he never held her hand at the opera. He never held her hand. Not once.

Chapter 6:
Revolving Door

The seasons come,
pass through.
An anticipation of blossoms
in the lemon trees.
Fresh seasoned emotion
can't stop dancing.

Still,
nature knows
when it's time
to ripen a heart.

Perhaps
every time is the right time.
To be loved,
you must give.

As the solstices
usher in the new,
at least
we are lucky to witness.
Be grateful to
all experiences.

It's still the photos I think of first when I think of Sam. After more than thirty years together, after raising two children, after so much love and caring, after so many memories both extraordinary and mundane, it's those photos that overflow my mind. Sometimes it's as if I'm still drowning in that cold saltwater feeling of my childhood.

Three decades is an impressive testament to love, to patience, or to weariness. For the first ten years, our life together was as normal as either of us could have expected. But when opportunity presented itself to him, I was set adrift on my emotions. Without reciprocation, I could only endure so long. Now I can see that even as I learned and grew through the years, Sam turned me inward again, the way I'd been as a little girl under my father's sharp shadow.

From the very beginning, Sam was unfailingly generous in every outward way. He bought me a new silver Mercedes, even as he continued to drive his own beat-up Honda. Fascinated by new technologies, he taught David computer skills at a time when such things were still rare. For David's tenth birthday, he gave him his first computer. When Mia was born, he bought a beautiful plot of land overlooking the bay, and together we designed a wonderful home for our family. It was only later that I recognized the sinister undertones of these generous acts, that it was all about maintaining control. He wanted to keep us all in the boxes he'd created for us. The one thing he could never be generous with was his emotions.

We lived together for almost six years before I was able to extract myself from the legal snarl of my marriage to Brian. Those were the calm, sun-dappled years of our love. After our wedding, when he had to return to New York for work, I wanted to come with him. We wanted another child, and I thought we should be together. But he insisted that I should stay in San Francisco, with David's school and his friends, with my work. But with Sam away and David in school, I began to grow restless.

From time to time, Sam and I walked to the little French restaurant around the corner from our house to enjoy a light meal. We got to know the owner and some of the other regular customers. One day, there was a notice pasted in the window. They were looking for a new, part-time chef.

I had no professional training, but plenty of experience. I'd taught myself to cook Sam's favorite French foods with Julia Child's books and her PBS series. Then I'd branched out to new cookbooks, more complicated recipes. I liked the delicate balance of French cooking, the sense of chemistry and artistry combined.

When I asked the owner, she agreed to give me a trial, despite my lack of experience. When she tasted my boeuf bourguignon, she hired me on the spot.

I loved the work. I was free to experiment, and I had the facilities and the capacity to perfect what I'd already learned. I became a minor sensation in the neighborhood, the Korean woman who made delicious French food. And I got to know the regulars.

One of these was a man named Roger, a middle-aged French man, a pioneering spirit who'd survived the horrors of the Second World War and come to the United States as an immigrant, like myself. The first time I met him, he came to the door of the kitchen to shake my hand.

"I never would have expected to taste such perfect French food prepared by a Korean chef!" He bowed and gave my hand a courtly kiss. "I wanted to tell you that I admire your spirit and determination."

From that day, Roger and I saw each other almost every week, when he came in for lunch. He liked to eat late, after the lunch rush, and by the time he'd finished his meal, he was often the only customer in the place. This gave me the opportunity to take a break with him, to sit down and share coffee and conversation.

I learned he'd been living in San Francisco most of his professional life. He was a neuroscientist, a professor at the university. His voice was gentle, enthusiastic. His whole demeanor exuded a sort of quiet admiration that I wasn't used to and didn't expect. I was charmed, delighted. He told me about his wife, his children, who were the same age as me. He wanted to know about my experiences, how I'd come to be in San Francisco. I was honest with him, as I was with everyone, and he received my story with open hands. From our very first conversation, all I had to do to earn his appreciation was to offer up my authentic self.

One spring evening, as we were cleaning up after the last customers had left, the owner asked me what I thought of Roger. I waxed enthusiastic.

"He is such a gentleman! So different from American men."

She nodded, smiling. "He's been coming here for years, ever since we opened." She wiped the wine glasses dry with a soft cloth. "Did you know he won a Nobel Prize in medicine?"

"Roger?" I blinked at her. "But he's such a humble, unpretentious man."

The owner smiled. "True. But also the kind of man who uses his research to make the world a better place. And never brags about it. That's why we love him."

Roger had a deep interest in contemporary art. When he found out I was a painter, he wanted to see my work, so I invited him to my home studio one evening. He exclaimed over the canvases, his clear eyes catching the depths of emotion, passion, and pathos he saw there. He pointed to openness, to courage in the face of judgment. We shared that attitude to life. As the months wore on, Roger became the mentor and friend I'd always longed for.

He thought my early experiences were a gift. He too had endured hardship at an early age, in the violence and privation of what he always referred to as the Great War. He'd worked in the French resistance, and even learned to speak fluent German. As a young woman, barely more than a girl, his wife had hidden their Jewish friends and helped them escape the Nazis. These hardships had battered and molded Roger into the man I admired so much. If he could turn his tragedies to inspiration, I would try to do the same. Roger woke me up. He gave me the jolt that would change my life.

As I built up my culinary reputation and cultivated my blossoming friendship with Roger, Sam began to resent my growing independence. After a happy year working at the restaurant, I discovered I was pregnant. Once again, I was torn between the plans I'd begun to make for myself and the knowledge of my responsibilities as a mother. I'd wanted another child so badly, but in the absence of a pregnancy, I'd found other pursuits to fill my time. And I knew I would miss them. But in the end, my children were the most important thing in my life. I was determined to give them the kind of childhood I would have wished for. When Sam suggested I should give up my job at the restaurant, I agreed.

This was another happy period for us. After Mia was born, we designed and built our new house together. The children had space to run and plenty of fresh air, and I had my own spacious studio. But with Sam away for longer and longer intervals, I effectively became a single mother. I was left alone to juggle the day-to-day duties of raising two children. I had less and less time for myself, for my art.

Even with all the advantages my marriage gave me, I was still first and foremost a foreigner. I'd given up my Korean passport to take US citizenship. But in San Francisco, I was always treated as a Korean. I would never fit in. Yet when I went back to Korea, even for brief visits, it was clear that I was a foreigner there as well. I floated over the world, never able to settle. It was liberating, but at times it was lonely and frustrating, too. And with Sam away in New York, I had to chart my own course. As my independence and my capacity to assert myself in my new home grew, Sam's tenderness shriveled.

Sam was always a loving father, when he was present. He was warm with his children in a way I never saw him with anyone else in his life. From the beginning, I knew he was introverted, that he would always rather spend time alone. For years I was the exception, his unconditional enabler, and it was easy for me to overlook his antisocial tendencies. But it was harder to ignore his inability to deal with change, with the unexpected. When I couldn't control all aspects of his environment, when I couldn't keep things constant and calm, he became paranoid. He retreated to his study and only came out for meals. At first, he maintained a calm façade in front of me, carefully controlling his reactions until he was alone. But as the years went by, it became impossible to ignore his lashing out. I exhausted myself trying to learn what would set him off, to anticipate and avert any event that might lead to an outburst. I found myself tiptoeing around him.

He insisted on a spotless house, military order. I decided to take the housekeeping into my own hands. I became an expert in every aspect of cleaning, attempting to control everything in his environment, to keep him calm. That pleased him, although it didn't turn the tide of his criticism. But even with his rigid demands for cleanliness and order, I was never allowed into his office. The glimpses I caught through the half-open door as he was closing it behind him revealed ziggurats of paper, books piled haphazardly on the floor-to-ceiling shelves, expensive works of art propped against chalky baseboards, dust floating through shafts of sunlight in the fetid air. I knew it was all a power play, but I extinguished my tentative flame of doubt. I wanted to love him, accept him, support him, even when his true colors began to clash with mine.

Our relationship worked in the beginning precisely because we were so different. We could have been completely complimentary, if we'd found a way to meet in the middle. I was an extrovert, used to accommodating and acclimated to constant change. Dealing with his disposition came naturally. At first, he offered me a kind of consistency and security I had craved all my life. After my father, after Brian's disappearance, all I wanted was someone who could maintain some sort of regularity and balance. Sam was steadfast. I was entirely confident he would never intentionally cause me pain, that he wouldn't suffer any breakdowns. He wasn't the type to run off to the woods or disappear one night and never come back. Sam was logical, straitlaced, and loyal. In other words, the opposite of the men I'd shared my life with up to that point. Our differences made the relationship exciting, gave us the independence to continue to grow together and as individuals.

I learned a lot from Sam. He was knowledgeable about food, wine, and music. I'd learned to cook French food because he loved it. He was a generous philanthropist. He donated to the San Francisco Opera and the Museum of Modern Art, to the Metropolitan Museum in New York. He introduced me to that world. I learned to appreciate the opera. We each took pleasure in supporting the arts we loved.

But everything changed in very slow motion. Like a kaleidoscope shifting, he turned from the quiet man I'd felt lucky to find into someone who was clearly suffering under the weight of some unnamed burden. It took many years for the cracks in his veneer to begin to show. I watched his body change shape, his jaw muscles clench, his neck thicken and sag. I listened to him complain that his tailor was incompetent, that his clothes didn't fit. I never suggested that it might be him who was changing. Nothing was ever his fault.

I have a clear memory of looking at him across the kitchen early one morning, as he was knocking back his second espresso before leaving for the airport. There were red circles all the way around his eyes. The skin around his mouth was dry and flaking. His clothes were stylish, as always, but the shirt under his jacket was rumpled, his shoes unpolished. He'd begun dying his hair a strange shade of brown that seeped into the skin around his temples. He didn't speak to me or even make eye contact. He just clinked his cup down, hefted his overnight bag, and marched out the door. I stood staring after him, thinking that this man was a stranger to me. He was not the man in the wedding photo I kept on the mantlepiece. This was someone else.

At first, I assumed it was something to do with his career. He never told me much about his professional life. I took that as par for the course in the secretive world of hedge fund management, submerged as it was in murky complexity. I assumed this world he carefully guarded from me was the origin of his allergy to transparency, his snarling defense of his privacy. I knew it was a high-pressure position, and I let that be the explanation for all the tension flowing off him and over our family in waves. He told me it was all boring, that I was better off in what he referred to as my "art world." He resented the time I spent painting and writing poetry. He didn't understand the emotion that went into it. For him, these were pointless pursuits, a waste of my time. He pushed me off into that sphere, and for the first time, I felt the icy cold that would come to characterize the barrier he was building between us, block by frigid block.

I watched as Sam detached himself from his children. I made sure they never wanted for anything I could provide. Perhaps because of his early experiences, David was always patient and adaptable. And Mia had never known a different life. She accepted warmth from her father when he offered it, but she learned to depend solely on me. It was me she ran to when she tripped on the stones in the garden, me who dried her tears. When Sam was home, he was gentle and attentive, and his children loved him. That made his absences more painful as time went on. But I was determined to break the negative cycle of my own upbringing, and I was gratified to watch my children grow. They each stood confidently at the center of their own lives, ready to give and forgive, patient with the failings of those they loved. And I learned from the resilience I saw modelled in my children, in their ability to adapt, in their hope.

Sam was an expert at making me doubt myself. As our marriage began to unravel, I would convince myself that he was suffering from depression, and then he would come home smiling, with a present for me, eager to spend the evening playing with our children. I would worry about his heavy drinking, and he would announce over breakfast that he was embarking on a two-week cleanse to purge his body, and would drink nothing but sparkling water. He would spend weeks in Manhattan, and my head would fill with visions of other women in the bed I'd picked out for his apartment, but then he would call me every night to tell me he loved me. Looking back, I still believe he meant those words every time he said them. But they were only one layer of our story. The secrets swirled under the surface.

I was never sure how many of his worries existed only in my imagination. But it was clear that we had lost our hold on each other. That he was drifting, and I had surrendered the will to continue swimming after him. He spent less and less time at home, and when he did return, he avoided my caresses, refused to touch me at all. I began sleeping in the guest room. He stopped making eye contact altogether. He began to grumble at his colleagues, at the other parents from the children's school whom I invited over for dinner, at our acquaintances from the opera and the modern art museum. No one was smart or sophisticated enough for him. He preferred not to talk to anyone at all rather than stoop to a level he considered beneath him.

I found myself more and more confused, by his behavior and his habits. The smallest noises or tics, the most inane phrases he uttered on a daily basis, things that had never bothered me before sent me into fits of annoyance that I could only cure by leaving the room. Yet I still believed it would get better. That we would identify the problem and be able to solve it, that we could move forward into something more mutual, solid and open. In the meantime, I took care of the children and spent all my extra energy on myself. I went back to my studio and poured myself into painting. I dug my old poetry notebooks out of the boxes I'd packed away before Mia was born. I hosted friends and school events, charity fundraisers and children's birthday parties. I built a world for myself, and I waited for Sam to look up and ask to join me there.

But he never did. So I found other things to throw myself into. We had two acres of land around the house we'd built together. I filled my internal void, my longing for growth and beauty, with hundreds of exotic plants, a collection of rare roses. When I could not sleep, I went out to work in the garden by moonlight. I bought a head-lamp. I worked so hard that my hands turned a whole different shade of brown than the rest of my body. Gardener's hands, Sam called them with his lip curled.

I started losing sleep. I began finding other ways to fill that dark, empty time. Keeping myself occupied constantly, with no room to reflect or consider alternatives. I began studying at night. French first, then German. The beautiful language of culture and art, of the food Sam and I both loved, and the intellectual language of the philosophers I'd fallen in love with as a girl. Sam's languages. I thought I was trying to please him, to draw him out into yet another space we might be able to inhabit together. Now, I wonder whether some part of me was already making an exit plan. Creating space for myself so that when the day came, when it all fell irrevocably apart, I would have options.

On the surface, my experience looked like the American dream. Even though I had exceeded all of my own expectations, I felt vulnerable living in that grand house in the San Francisco hills, with a handsome, stimulating, sophisticated man and warm-hearted children. All my life, I had embraced vulnerability as my greatest strength. Now that I had every outward reason to feel secure, I couldn't shake the feeling that this life was too good to be true. Sam was not happy. He wanted novelty. He was pushing me away. Cold and solitary, he made me keenly aware of the cruel artifice of my life. I was outwardly successful, outwardly happy, but I was not free. What would happen if I opened my heart even more?

It took me a long time to realize I wanted to leave that world. Everything everyone assumed I should want was stifling me. I found myself dreaming of the temple, of the bright mountain air, the simple food, the stabilizing rituals, even the simple grey robes. I wondered what my life would have been like if I had clung to that place. But I have always believed that the only direction I can go in life is forward. Regret serves no purpose. I knew I wanted to walk out of that huge house into a different life. But by that time, I had been with Sam for half my life. It had become increasingly hard to remember a time when he was not there. We had built a home together, something I had never had but always longed for. And I wanted to give my children the stability I had craved as a child. It was impossible to find my path out. I thought of Mr. Kim, the teacher who had mentored me. I thought of my sister. And I felt I had failed them.

Sam was pushing me as he'd once pushed precious objects to the edge of shelves to watch them teeter. He wanted to see when I would break. I lasted much longer than he'd anticipated. I was made of stronger stuff. But once I was finally pushed from my luxurious ledge, my life was put back in motion. As it broke into pieces, I found long-lost parts of myself, and I learned how to glue it all back together into a structure I could inhabit.

The first time I found him out, it was not the death blow to our marriage, the way I had always assumed that type of revelation must be. My own acquiescence surprised me. I was too invested in enabling him. My pain, past and present, wasn't enough to catapult me out of my own bad habits.

Sam was spending the weekend in New York. More and more often, this was his routine. When he missed his usual Friday night call, I wondered, but I didn't worry. We'd been drifting apart, and I thought he might need his space. I knew he was busy. But when I still didn't hear from him on Saturday night, I became concerned. I tried the phone in his apartment, but it rang and rang into empty space. I tried his office, but it was the weekend, and of course nobody picked up. I called all through the night. By Sunday morning, I was frantic. What if he'd had an accident? What if he'd collapsed somewhere? I thought of heart attacks, strokes. I called every hospital in New York, gave them his name, his description. I called the police. A bored voice in a Manhattan precinct told me it was too soon to declare him missing, then hung up. I thought of Brian, all those years ago. Of the sheriff who'd taken pity on me. I'd always been so sure Sam was incapable of disappearing. Had I been wrong?

I left the children with one of David's friends and rushed to the airport. I was determined to be on the next available flight to New York. I'd look for him myself. I'd scour the hospitals, search every face. While I waited to board the plane, I called the apartment again. Sam picked up. I sagged against the wall, my knees so weak that I had to sit down on the dirty terminal floor.

"Hana! How are you?"

I choked out a cry.

"Is anything wrong?"

I closed my eyes, took three deep breaths.

"I've been calling all weekend. I was frantic. I thought—" I hesitated, trying to frame my worries in words. "I thought something must have happened to you."

"Don't be ridiculous. What could happen?"

"You didn't call!" I wailed. "Where were you?"

The line hissed with a suggestive silence. Finally he spoke, his voice calm, collected.

"Where are you right now?"

"I'm at the airport! I was getting on the next plane to New York. To find you."

"Go home." It sounded like an order. "Go home, Hana. I'll call you there."

But when he called, it was to tell me he'd be on the next flight to San Francisco. And when he arrived, he sat me down on the sofa, stood on the other side of the room, and made a speech he'd clearly rehearsed. About how he'd hired a woman for sex. It was recent, he said. It had only happened a few times.

"It's only natural, with me being away so much."

I stared, open mouthed.

"Are you in love with her?"

He gave a bitter laugh. "Of course not. I love you. This is just sex. It means nothing."

"It means something to me!"

We were both quiet, fallen in on ourselves like bombed-out buildings. The light began to fade from the windows overlooking the Concubine Garden. Finally he spoke.

"Maybe I need help."

"You mean like a marriage counsellor?"

He nodded. I had to take him at his word. The children were still young. David would be leaving for college in a year. Mia was nine. They needed a stable environment. I thought I could hold myself together, give him time to sort things out.

The counsellor suggested individual therapy. In my first session with the psychiatrist, he told me gently but firmly that I was a doormat. A professional enabler. I studied the horizon of my life, and it was hard to argue with his assessment. But it was even harder to envision a different way to be. Sam came home from his sessions and presented the results in single words and pop-culture jargon. Stress. Depression. Sex addiction. I thought these were the stems and leaves of his problem, not the roots.

The psychiatrist prescribed him a cocktail of medications, and his libido waned. He blamed the drugs. I sympathized, comforted. I resigned myself to the fact that he never touched me anymore. Not to express desire, or even simple affection. I let him pack me away. I made myself small.

I was still the perfect enabler. Neither of us had learned anything.

I don't know how I ever could have found the strength to detach myself from that life if it hadn't been for the art and poetry that had sparked the flame of resilience in me since I was a child. I used creativity as a path to think outside my box and interact with the negative energies swirling around me. This gift gave me comfort and, little by little, reinforced the strength I needed to create positive emotions and outcomes. Art is my still pond. It has given me insight into myself from an early age, steered me through my darkest moments. As a child, painting and poetry buoyed my search for alternatives to abuse and despair. Knowledge was a ladder, first to bring me down into my core, and then to lift me out of my situation. Artistic experimentation was one of the primary ways I acquired the knowledge I needed to save myself.

But creativity was not something I could control. It came and went. Sometimes it filled me until I overflowed onto paper or canvas. Other times I went searching for it, deep down in that old blue cavern, only to climb back up empty-handed. Those were some of the heaviest moments of my life. Gradually, I learned how to create the conditions for creativity to visit. I learned to allow myself to feel deeply, to look down into the depths as I desperately treaded water, to accept the turmoil even as I refused to let it pull me under. I learned to rely on myself. To get up early and spend time in my studio, alone. Not to be ruled by fatigue or hunger. As my children grew and left home, I was less tied to their schedules, free to pursue these twin creative avenues. To sit in the garden in the early morning and write. To get my hands dirty planting and pruning, to let the paint cover my clothes, my skin. To visualize deep emotion for others to see. To share myself in this way, when other paths were blocked. After years of thrashing in the swells, I finally rediscovered the lifeline that had always led me to shore in the past. And it reliably pulled me back again, although this time in a different direction.

With the tension in the house no longer cut by the sharp young voices of my children and their friends, I poured myself into painting and poetry, gardening and cooking, as a way to relieve stress and refocus my mind. I was surprised when people outside this solitary world began to notice. At first friends and acquaintances, then art connoisseurs and even a few galleries. I sold a painting, and then a few more. At the end of a year of this frantic creative eruption, Roger approached me with a proposition.

Roger and I had continued our friendship even after I left the restaurant. We no longer saw each other every week, but we talked on the phone often, and his family welcomed me warmly into their circle. We gave each other support, mutual appreciation and affection. The more I got to know him, his wife, and their five children, the more they impressed me. Every family struggles, but they had found a way to avoid hurting each other in the long process of love and life. They had a peace I had long been reaching for in my own life. This was the kind of world I wanted to create for my children, the kind of support and protection I sought to offer them through those difficult years.

When Roger bought his first Macintosh computer in the 1980s, it was for scientific research purposes. But then he stumbled upon the Macpaint program and was drawn into experimenting with digitally manipulating images. He was intrigued by the chance to paint without canvas or dye. But being an artist, he told me, turned out to be much more difficult than winning Nobel prizes. Nevertheless, Roger was one of the first pioneers in digital art, and local gallerists were noticing.

One of them had invited Roger to launch a solo exhibition. He'd considered it, and then approached the gallerist with an idea. He thought it would be better to put together a joint exhibition. With me.

I had never expected a breakthrough like this. When I told Sam, he shrugged off all my excitement. He'd never been enthusiastic about the time I spent on creative work, and at the beginning of our relationship, I'd gradually let it slip into the background. After I found him out the first time, as I invested more and more of the energy he'd rebuffed into artistic work, he became more and more disparaging. It was one way he tried to keep me in the box he'd constructed for me. But there were others who were waiting to offer help when I began to break free.

As we planned the exhibition, Roger refused to put any information about his awards or his Nobel Prize on his art, resisting the protests of the gallery owner, who knew the market value of such a distinction. I saw in him the courage to thwart the competitive spirit that destroys so many people, that was devouring Sam.

But I began to feel the old insecurity in the pit of my stomach, the anxiety and confusion of the lonely little girl who'd hidden in the school bathroom, who didn't think herself worthy to put on an exhibit with such a well-known scientist, someone who had spent his life improving the world. But Roger reassured me with his usual authenticity and lack of pretension. In the end, the exhibition was a modest success, a great unexpected gift from my mentor. It set my feet on a new path.

Roger became my anchor. In the process of cutting myself free from Sam, of freefalling off the cliff of my former life towards the waves below, of finding my feet on solid ground again, I felt that Roger was the only man who understood me. He might have been the father I'd always needed. He and his family always offered me unconditional acceptance. But it was more than that. He turned me away from myself and back towards the world, and I found my sense of inspiration again.

My friendship with Roger revived the open vulnerability I'd once shared with my sister, the kind of transparent connection I hadn't felt with anyone since I came to the States. I'd offered it to Brian and been abandoned. In the aftermath of that hurt, I'd closed myself off from Jim. I'd tried to open myself to Sam, but he'd rejected me, and each year felt colder and more cruel than the last. Roger was a source of love and light.

I was fortunate to have people at every stage of my life who wanted to protect me, to give me a hand to raise me up out of the waves and onto solid ground. Once again I felt connected, supported, safe. Roger was the latest and the best of these men, and without him, I may never have been able to pick up the pieces of my world when it finally shattered under the pressure.

As I built up my self-confidence again, I realized just how much I had lost in my marriage. Sam had taken many things from me, but I'd also been willing to give myself away, over and over again. As I put the pieces back together and raised my authentic self like a sunken ship from the ocean floor, I began to feel trapped in my life with Sam. As if he was boring holes faster than I could patch them. For years, I'd seen myself as a devoted wife and mother. Roger was flabbergasted by the consent with which I punished myself. He had no sympathy for the despair that was constantly threatening to drown me, to wash away all my creative work. He had no patience for floundering. He looked at my new paintings, he read my latest poetry, and he told me I had all the energy I needed to create my own solution. He was the first person in my life honest enough to tell me that I could have no happiness if I stayed with Sam.

"We learn from our mistakes, or we sink."

He turned from the view out the window of my studio, laid an arm gently across my shoulders.

"You have a choice, Hana. It's a clear question of survival."

But Roger was not the only man who breathed into my life during those difficult years.

I first met Hélie on the evening of my fiftieth birthday. I was in Paris with my family to celebrate. But the trip, like my two decades of marriage, was sliding into one long disappointment.

Sam was due to go to Paris on business, and as a birthday surprise, he bought tickets for me and the children. We were all delighted with his spontaneity. We boarded the plane smiling and laughing, looking like the happy family I still hoped we would turn out to be. Sam whisked us to the hotel, then left to take care of business. He didn't return. I had a beautiful, decadent suite all to myself, and it began to feel like a microcosm of my life. As the day of my birthday approached, I counted down the hours, hoping he would join us. I wandered the early summer streets with my children, past the fountains at Place de la Concorde and into the cool shade of the Tuileries. I found myself wondering who it was all for. Sam returned late that night and left early in the morning, complaining of exhaustion.

I struggled to keep my equilibrium. Something about this beautiful foreign city, the gorgeous food and the musical language, pushed me off balance. My children tried hard not to mention their father's strange behavior, and I never discussed our problems with them. They encouraged me into galleries and fine restaurants. They were well acquainted with my fascination with French food. They'd been devouring my pastries, foie gras, and carré d'agneau for years. On the night before my birthday, Sam failed to turn up. My children convinced me to join them for dinner at a small restaurant close to the hotel, a simple place the concierge had told them served the best coq au vin in the city. I was depressed, reluctant to go, but I appreciated their thoughtfulness. When we arrived, I was delighted at the authentic, humble food, and determined not to let Sam's absence spoil their sweet gesture.

The tables were crammed close together, draped in white linen, flanked by red leather bench seats that ran from one end of the wood-paneled room to the other. By sputtering candlelight we laughed and told old stories, not knowing who was eavesdropping at the next table. Hélie and his friend Pierre, whom the waiters greeted like old friends, heard us discussing my birthday. As we debated which wine to order, Hélie leaned over the narrow space between our tables and suggested in perfect English something that would complement our simple meal. We took his advice, and then fell into conversation. He learned about our trip, where we came from. He told us he'd lived in Washington DC for a few years. When Mia asked what he did there, he was modest.

"In my younger days, I was a diplomat."

We talked about the places we'd traveled, about American culture and politics. We talked for hours, until the restaurant was empty and the waiters began to blow out the candles on the neighboring tables.

As we got up to leave, Hélie helped me into my coat.

"Are you staying nearby? Shall I call you a taxi?"

Before I could say anything, David piped up.

"No need. We're right next door."

As we stepped out into the soft summer air and that particular pink Parisian light, Hélie bowed and gave me his card with both hands. A simple creamy card, printed with just his name and telephone number.

"If you need anything during your stay, please don't hesitate to call."

The next morning, my birthday, Sam's side of the bed was cold and empty. I laid awake until the maid knocked on the door, carrying a vase of three dozen pink roses, with a card attached. I ripped it open and my eyes flew first to the name at the bottom, hoping against instinct and experience that such a gesture would have come from Sam. But it was Hélie's name at the bottom. I couldn't stop the tears welling, and they overflowed all through the morning while I hid in my room, sunk in the claw-footed bathtub, staring out at a grey shrouded sky. Sam had not even come back to the room last night. I wondered what other personal interests he was pursuing in Paris.

As I dressed to meet my children for lunch, I tossed Hélie's card into the gilded waste paper basket under the desk. I had no doubt his gesture was kindly meant, but it depressed me. I assumed that Sam was having his own liaison in another part of the city. I thought of that day at the airport, waiting for news from New York, of the terrible weight of Sam's announcement. It would be easy to give myself permission to take a lover. But the idea of retaliation in kind held no charm for me. I was overwhelmed by loneliness.

Yet all through lunch, I couldn't stop thinking about the elegant, charming man I'd met the night before. In my mind, I played over and over my complaints to Sam about the lack of intimacy in our relationship, and his repeated insistence that I should find myself a lover. That I should pursue what I needed elsewhere. I knew Sam simply wanted to normalize his own behavior, to encourage me into the same kind of infidelity he had seized for himself with both hands. And I'd always rejected this as a solution. But Hélie intrigued me. When I got back to my room, I dug his card out of the trash. I was so tired of waiting for love, for intimacy. I was tempted.

Hélie's voice came warm and brimming down the line. If he was surprised to hear from me, he gave no sign.

"If you are still free, I'd be honored to invite you and your children to dinner tonight. To celebrate."

We made plans to meet for dinner at Alain Ducasse, at the Plaza Athénée. But my children declined. They encouraged me to go out and enjoy myself. They didn't mention their father, but I knew they were also upset.

When I arrived at the restaurant and saw Hélie across the room, I was flooded with warmth. He rose to greet me, kissed my hand. He was a few years older than me, and it was clear that he appreciated style. He was well-dressed, in understated, natural fibers, elegantly tailored. His style and demeanor made me think of Roger. He complimented the elegance of my attire, telling me my clothes were perfectly to his taste. I watched the way the eyes of other diners, men and women, drifted to our table, to Hélie's face. It was not only I who was charmed by his charisma.

He told me more about his life in the States. He played down his professional life, but it was clear he was a natural leader, that he'd taken on many challenges. Yet he was open about mistakes he'd made, and he had no trouble laughing at the stories he told about himself. I responded with my usual openness, and I felt the glow refracting between us. At the end of the meal, I told him how much he reminded me of Roger. Then I worked up my courage to ask the question that had been circling our table all evening.

"Why did you send me those roses?"

He studied me for a moment before he answered.

"As a diplomat, I learned how to take care of people. When I heard you talking last night." He hesitated, observing my reaction. "When I learned your husband hadn't showed up on your birthday, I felt for you. I thought you deserved to have a nice evening."

I realized with a start that Hélie was just like me. The kind of person who takes other people's problems on his shoulders, who feels deep empathy. I was touched by his generous consideration. But I was too afraid to ask for more. To ask whether he was married, what he saw in me. It was a beautiful evening, and that was enough.

"Thank you," I said simply.

Hélie walked me to my taxi, kissed my cheek.

"I hope to see you soon."

Back in San Francisco, I heard from him from time to time. He sent emails, occasionally he called. He wanted to know where I was, what I was doing. He asked when I was coming back to Paris. All along, I was longing for someone. But for the moment, that unfulfilled longing, that shimmering possibility, was enough.

The shock of my final discovery of Sam's bizarre behavior still lurks in my muscle memory. When the images I saw on the screen that afternoon rise to my mind, I feel the tingling in my hands, the heavy weight pulling my head to earth. The stone in my chest.

But it was not the betrayal itself that pushed me into the leap I needed to take to save myself. It was not the sex, not the years of hiding and lying. It was not the knowledge that Sam had pushed my warm affection away and sought a different kind of heat in other beds. It was not the number of women he confessed to hiring over the years, not the way he'd objectified and abused them. It was not even his suggestion that we could stay together, could even be happy, if only I would accept his flings and pursue affairs of my own. These were terrible revelations. That long look into the depths of his tangled mind pushed me against the wall and held me there, struggling to breathe. But what gave me the strength to break free, to jump, was the realization that I'd lost myself somewhere in his mess. That in spite of all the terrible things he'd done to me, some of which I had even suspected over the years, I had allowed him to make me small. To squeeze me into the compartment he'd created for me. I knew there was nothing I had done or not done to deserve this. I never thought his problems were my fault. Yet I had fallen so easily back into the patterns of the little girl I'd been under my father's roof. I had lost my octopus and become once again the solitary stone.

In the end, this realization is what gave me the strength to stand up. To stop shouting. To calmly tell Sam that he should go to New York, take time to think about what he wanted to do with our marriage. It was this vision I held before my eyes when I stood looking at the long, still pond in front of our house, the one Sam had modelled on the Garden of the Concubines, and suddenly felt I'd gone blind. I spent time with my children, with Roger and his family. I realized that what Roger saw in me was precisely those pieces of myself that I'd gradually lost sight of in my years with Sam. They'd been hidden, dormant, but he saw them, glittering like gold nuggets at the bottom of a rushing stream. They were still there. I could be the octopus again. I could use my many talents to put myself back together.

All through that difficult time, Hélie continued to call. In my dim cloud of grief, I was too broken to trust. Another romance was not what I needed. I couldn't see the point of putting myself through the same pain again. Roger had given me the courage to turn my gaze in another direction, and I followed that sun as it gradually began to shimmer through the fog. I built myself up again, determined to reopen to the world without giving myself away. That blossoming seeped into my conversations with Hélie. But still I resisted.

Once, just before we hung up, he asked me a question that caught me unprepared.

"What is the most important thing in your life?"

I thought of my children. I thought of my art. I thought of Brian and Sam, Jim and Roger. I thought of the childhood I'd worked so hard to escape. I tried to string it all together like beads on a necklace, reaching for what all those things had in common.

"Unconditional love," I told him at last. And I was sure I could hear him smile down the line.

"You are always right."

Gently, I hung up the phone.

Looking back on that day, I think I'd like to change

my answer. The most important thing in my life has been and will always be resilience.

And I would need it again, sooner than I could have imagined.

Chapter 7:
Another Convincing Kiss

What do we know?
Our aching hearts never slept.
Let's blame it
on human magnetism.

Or
a labyrinth of instincts.
Certainly
it wasn't a passing limerence.

Yet
it wheels away
on the whirlwind.
We should have known.

Perhaps
another convincing kiss
will tell
our whole story.

It seems Hans has always been searching for perfection.

Lübeck sparkled that summer. Everything was light and water, red-tiled roofs and cobblestone streets. It was in this shimmering June that he met Hana.

They were each taking refuge from their past. They were both buried, desperately trying to scratch their way out into some bigger, better, brighter future that neither of them could fully visualize. The sunshine gave them hope, but the shadows of skimming summer clouds called up separate feelings of loss for each of them.

Hana was a guest at the summer home of one of her collectors, an hour outside of Hamburg. Christian was building up his family's collection of modern art, hoping to launch a small private museum in town. He'd met Hana through their mutual friend Roger and invited her to stay for the summer as an artist-in-residence. Christian was also the trustee of a medical research program, and he had invited several of his colleagues to his home for a long weekend.

When Hans received the invitation, he argued with himself about whether to go. It would be good for business. And good for him to get out of the whirlpool he was stuck in after the wreck of his marriage. He was out of his depth. He hated that lonely, thrashing feeling. Knowing he had failed. Part of him wanted to pull the curtains, curl into a ball, and see no one, say nothing. But he could not stand to be left out. To miss an opportunity. He forced himself to go.

The lights strung across the garden shone gold in the electric blue twilight. Candles sputtered on the tables, crystal and silver glinted. The lake lapped the end of the dock at the foot of the long lawn, a pleasant sound that drew Hans to the water's edge, away from the hum of conversation.

The food was exquisite. Salmon with garlic and hot pepper, served over homemade calamari ink pasta. It had been a long time since he'd put something in his mouth and savored it. His swirling thoughts slowed, and he chewed deliberately. The words swimming through the air around him drained from his ears, and he focused on his plate. A moment of clarity, of simplicity, one that remained etched in his memory long after that summer faded.

Maybe he'd had one glass of wine too many. Maybe it was the feeling of being adrift, cut loose from the relationships that had once anchored his life. Maybe it was the laughter ringing too loudly in his ears. As the other guests pushed their chairs back from the table, lit cigarettes and emptied wine bottles into tapering glasses, he went in search of the kitchen. To say thank you.

He expected to be greeted by a team. Instead he found a single woman, working steadily on a series of triangular dessert plates adorned with bright raspberry tarts. Dwarfed by the gleaming steel and bright white ceiling, her black bobbed hair tilted forward at an angle that hid her face. Her hands flicked across the counter with quick precision, splitting mint leaves, spooning cream. His mind staggered under the meal and the wine. He couldn't connect her with the food he'd eaten. But the sharp scent of spearmint filled his nostrils, cleared his head.

She glanced up with her head on one side, casting a knife-edge of shadow across her face. He expected German, but a lilting English tumbled out instead.

"Are you looking for me?"

It seemed he was.

"I've just come to thank the chef for the masterful meal."

They were both surprised.

"Oh, thank you. I always like to hear when people are pleased with my cooking."

"Did you do all this by yourself?" It was the first and last time he would doubt her determination.

"Yes." Her voice was matter-of-fact, if a little sheepish. "I used to teach cooking. I love to cook, and Herr von Bergstein has been so generous to me. It seemed like a nice way to thank him."

Her hands never stilled. In the silence that followed, it occurred to him it was rude not to ask if she needed help. She put him to work drizzling sauce and sprinkling toasted almonds. It took several plates for him to perfect the technique.

Together they loaded the trays that then sailed out onto the lawn on the upraised palms of the domestic staff. She dusted her hands matter-of-factly and untied her apron. She brushed off the glass of wine he offered to pour for her with a wave of her hand.

"Thank you, but I don't drink."

He thought better of having another drink himself.

Standing in the kitchen, leaning on the sugardusted counter, they discovered each other. He learned that she was American, that she'd been born in Korea. That she was an artist. That she'd be turning sixty in two weeks. That she was alone. That she felt a bit lost in the tides of German medical talk, but at home in this brightly lit kitchen.

He gaped at her, but she didn't laugh.

"You're surprised I've told you so much so fast?" Her eyes, focused on his hand propped on the countertop, seemed to lighten. "I always try to answer any question bluntly and honestly. It saves time."

He studied her hands as she studied his. Her nails were short, unpolished. Her skin was tanned.

"You look like someone who's used to working with her hands."

"Painting, cooking, gardening in the California sun." She held up her palms and nodded. "My hands are my best tools."

She looked him in the eye for the first time and asked about him. Quietly and directly. They drifted out into the garden, wandering from one potted plant to the next. He noted the paralysis on one side of her face, the fact that his noticing didn't seem to bother her. He admired her confidence, her self-possession. And he told her his story in a way that put his own life in order for him.

As the lights dimmed and the other guests drifted into the house, they sat on the terrace in the dark and talked on. The midsummer solstice light was just beginning to fade from the sky. He realized how late it must be. He said he should probably go up to his room. He didn't want to.

She nodded, told him it had been nice meeting him. They walked to the back door, where their host was waiting to wish them both goodnight. Hans held her hand for a moment longer than politeness dictated. He lingered without any clear intent. He blurted that he'd like to see her work. She chuckled, told him it was too late for that. She offered to give him a tour of her studio the next morning.

When he came down the stairs in the morning, Hana was already waiting in the garden. Most of the other guests were still asleep. Christian was making coffee in the kitchen, the buzz of the machine drifting over the grass like bees. She and Hans were alone. She led him to the little former boathouse at the edge of the trees where she'd set up her studio.

The light fell through the door in one long triangle, illuminating the explosions of color on the plain pine walls. The emotion in her paintings was raw but refined. Just what he felt in her presence, even after so few hours together. She gestured, waited silently for his reaction. He could appreciate art, and he knew enough to hold up his end of a conversation at a dinner party, but he worried that he had no insight to share about what he saw before him. He felt like he'd just emerged from a spin, his own unstable emotional weight throwing him off balance. He saw passion, joy, and calm contentment. But somehow sorrow, the one emotion he'd been drowning in for months, was absent. He hesitated as she studied him, then spoke his thoughts aloud. She nodded as if his assessment made perfect sense.

"There is no sorrow in pathos," she said. "That's the title of the painting. I painted it just after I turned fifty." She turned to him. "I believe you can feel deeply without losing yourself."

They stood in comfortable silence for a few more moments, contemplating her words as they drifted out into the bright morning.

"Come to Berlin," he blurted. She turned to him with surprise. "Berlin is the perfect place to create. It's inspiring. The history, the energy." He turned to her canvases. "You must see it. I'd be happy to give you a tour."

"I've been to Berlin," she said mildly. She told him she'd visited shortly before the wall came down, as part of an art project she'd been involved in, collecting the stories of people living in the East. "It was a difficult place. Pressed flat under those grey clouds."

"But it's different now," he insisted. "It's a whole different city. Everything has changed. You really must see it."

She agreed to come the next weekend. He picked her up at the station and they toured the streets on foot. They wandered through Mitte, the heart of the city, crossing back and forth between the old East and the old West. He took her to galleries and shops, walking along Unter den Linden, through the Brandenburg Gate. She was fascinated by the energy all around. He watched her eyes dart from face to face, take in the graffiti, the cafés, the uneven cobblestone streets, empty lots next to neoclassical buildings next to bright new steel and glass offices. He saw her drinking it in. He knew Berlin was already tightening its hold on her, as it had on him.

In the evening, she had to catch her train back to Hamburg. But he insisted on treating her to an early dinner. He took her to a trendy, expensive restaurant near the twin churches of Gendarmenmarkt. They ate by candlelight, talked about what they each wanted from life. He was already thinking that Hana could be precisely what he needed. She wanted a fresh start, she said. A place to focus on her art, a place of inspiration. She didn't feel at home in Germany, but she could already see that Berlin was different. She wanted calm, the peace of contentment rather than the passionate chaos her last marriage had been. She made it clear that she was not looking for a man. But as she talked, it became clear to Hans that he was looking for someone just like her.

When the bill came, he busied himself with his phone. He let her pick it up and pay for both of them. Over his protests, she got into a taxi in front of the restaurant and sped off to the station to catch the late train. But not before he'd extracted a promise that she would spend the next weekend with him in Berlin.

He invited her to his apartment. For a simple meal, he told her. He wanted to introduce her to the German tradition of Abendbrot – cold salami, black bread, and a salad. It was the first time she'd tasted German food like this, and the idea of cold food for dinner left her chilled. But she was gracious. She offered to make Korean food for him sometime. She commented on the bare white walls, the lack of furniture. He told her he'd come to Berlin with just two suitcases, clutching all his remaining possessions. He'd started over with so little, but he was slowly rebuilding, taking the time to discover what he really wanted in the process. She was delighted with the simplicity of the idea. So he challenged her.

"How would you like to try it? Could you move here with just two suitcases?"

She turned to study him. He realized he was holding his breath.

"I'd need my paintings," she said. "That's more than two suitcases."

He pulled her into a sudden embrace, held her so tight he heard her gasp.

"I suppose we could make an exception."

On the night of their very first meeting, a feeling of total comprehension is what kept him up talking until two in the morning. That feeling revived and intensified every time she came to see him in Berlin the rest of that summer. He wanted nothing more than to spend his life in a series of those conversations. But he had already committed to joining Doctors Without Borders in the Amazon for several months in the autumn. It was the realization of a youthful dream. It would give him the chance to do some good. But after knowing Hana for just a few short months, he felt helpless. He had known right away that he needed her. But he didn't want to give up any of his chances. He was at another crossroads, unsure which path to take.

He decided to be stern with himself. He went. But

he suffered. His pining for Hana started as soon as he arrived in Brazil, and it hit him much harder than he'd expected. It became a painful, daily craving. Sleeping in a bunk bed, accosted by the constant hum of mosquitos, he amused himself with fantasies of what a life with Hana might be like. As he lay awake at night, he began to talk to her aloud until he fell asleep. She became his obsession.

Desire is the most intense emotion. After a month, he was too restless to concentrate. It was all too much. He asked for permission to leave for a couple of weeks, just to see her again. It was a desperate attempt to ease his mind enough to continue the work. But he was refused in no uncertain terms. The organization had too much experience with doctors leaving and never returning. From that point on, lovesickness gnawed at him physically, as though he had contracted the kind of virus he was supposed to be treating. He couldn't eat or sleep. He lost weight, he became weak. He no longer had the energy to treat his patients. He wanted nothing more than to see Hana. Everything else faded into insignificance. He gave in. He packed his bags and returned to Berlin.

For him, it was settled from that moment. At the end of the summer, when he left Germany for South America, Hana had returned to San Francisco. They'd been in contact since then, but the internet connection in the Amazon was unreliable. He sent her an email telling her he was on his way back, and when he landed in Frankfurt, he opened his mailbox, half expecting a message saying she'd be on the next plane to Berlin. But there was nothing.

Hana took longer to ponder the decision. She discussed it with her children, her friends. She spent time walking, painting and writing, while he waited in his empty apartment in Berlin. In his mind, he'd already started to refer to the place as theirs. Each of those days was agony. One moment he was confident she would come, the next he was terrified she wouldn't.

In the end, she came with two suitcases. Crates of her artwork came later, adding the first color to his bare white walls. From the beginning, Hans held Hana as tightly as he dared. Every day for seven years, they followed the daily rituals he initiated. He adopted Hana's habit of taking a bath each morning and ending the day with another in the evening. They savored meals side by side, because he preferred to sit next to her. They went together to the bakery every morning. When she went to do the grocery shopping, he came along. If she wanted to go out for a walk, he would follow. He wanted these rituals to strengthen the emotional and physical intimacy they had both missed in their previous relationships. In his affection for her, he was also protecting himself. Creating attachment. He wrapped himself up in her so he would never again have to face his loneliness. He needed her to support him.

Hans felt that Hana had arrived in his life at the perfect moment. And he wanted access to all of her. He wanted to visit every part of her mind, her body, wherever and whenever he was driven to go. He craved being nearer in the same way he craved food when he was hungry or wine at the end of a long day. He couldn't fall asleep unless he was holding her hand. He clung to their rituals, believing they embodied the sort of cleansing both he and Hana needed, washing away the exhaustion, the sediment of each of their previous relationships. He felt as if they were past lovers, reunited by chance, or perhaps by intuition.

Hans envisioned Hana as someone who had pierced the veil and found that other energy, that extra intuition that so many people educate away. And he felt that she understood him in a deep, visceral way. She knew the particular pain of feeling alone in a marriage, lonely in what should be the most intimate of relationships. She was creative and intense. Full of ideas. He wanted to insert himself into her vision. After the marriage he'd been catapulted out of, he thought Hana was more than a miracle. She was the perfect partner.

Almost.

Hans met his first wife, Kerstin, when they were still children, through family connections. But it wasn't until after university that anything more than friendship grew up between them. She had always been the glowing girl who inspired a sort of awe in others, and she recognized that and knew how to use it. The two of them were familiar but not close, not even after their relationship bloomed into romance. They built their love around nostalgia, around that glow she was so good at projecting.

Kerstin was completely overpowering, not afraid to say anything, and her daring captivated Hans. He had returned home fresh from medical school, quite proud of his achievements, with the sort of runaway confidence of someone who has yet to be worn down by the world. She came from a privileged family, and Hans wanted a privileged life. Wealthy, cultured, and secure. He'd been brought up next to that world, by people who wanted to be part of it. His family had always pushed him to act as if he belonged there. So he focused on becoming who she thought he should be.

Over more than twenty years of marriage, they had three children together. Hans had always wanted the stability of a big family, and the children were the bond that held him and Kerstin together. He clung not just to her, but to the world she represented. She was his way in.

But Kerstin began to drift away. She loved their children, but she looked forward to the time when they would be grown, when she could pursue her own life again. Hans could never understand that. He wanted another child, another link in the chain. But she was adamant that she did not want more children. She started avoiding sex, bringing home literature about vasectomy. He refused to even consider the idea. He threw his frenzied energy into the marriage, did everything in his power to mold their relationship back into the shape it had when they were happy. He wanted to keep her close. He tried to interest her in making love every day. But the connection had lost its spark. As he clung to her, she distanced herself. She spent more and more time with her own friends. When they went out, it was always with other couples. She resisted being alone with him. Increasingly, that lack of intimacy and support made Hans physically sick. As she pushed him away, he tried to hold her tighter.

When she finally insisted the relationship was over, he was devastated. He screamed, cried. He begged for another chance, for another child. But she was impervious to all his pleading. She asked him to leave their home. She cut him adrift. He had no choice but to accept it. All the loneliness she'd helped him hold at bay came rushing back. He couldn't forgive her for that.

He decided he would reinvent himself. He would start something new, with someone new. When the divorce papers came, it was like a breath of frigid winter air, refreshing and bracing, burning and painful all in the same moment. She kept the house she'd bought for them, took custody of their three kids. He left two decades of marriage with the contents of two suitcases and not much more. He moved to Berlin. He arrived as the city was just beginning to recreate itself, reeling, yet feeling all the excitement of that rare opportunity to start over again.

But it wasn't the first time he'd been launched into a new existence with his entire world contained in a suitcase clutched in his hand.

Hans has always loved train travel. Sitting quietly and

watching the scenery flash by. But every time the train cruises into a tunnel, he feels an overwhelming anxiety that the whole thing might collapse. Of course, the train always comes through just fine, but he feels the same anxiety as soon as it reaches the next tunnel. He can't tell whether that fear is a memory or a premonition.

He remembers very little of his parents. Sometimes he sees flashes of his mother's colorful clothes, her red coat; sometimes he smells the worn leather of his step-father's black medical bag, feels the stethoscope knocking against his chest, hears the sound of his own heartbeat in his ears.

It happened on a trip to visit one of his step-father's friends in northern Germany. Hans has no memory of that day, but he's been told the story so many times that he feels as if he can hear the screeching tires, smell the leaking gasoline. They'd been traveling on a narrow road. Maybe his step-father was driving too fast. Maybe it was raining. Their car collided with a truck head on, and rolled. Sometimes he's still jerked out of sleep in the middle of the night, imagining he can feel the seatbelt digging into his chest as he hangs upside-down in the back of the car. He sees the spreading cracks in the windshield, the roof of the car dented in, just inches from his head. But he never sees his parents. There is no last vision of them, no slumping silhouette, no bloodied star on the broken glass.

His last real memory of his parents is domestic, commonplace. He sees them at home, right before they got in the car that day. His mother in the kitchen, calling out picnic items to be included in the basket for the trip. His step-father too busy with his newspaper to respond to her suggestions. And then in a flurry, they were out the door, his step-father packing the trunk as Hans strained to lift the suitcases one by one. His mother bundled him into the back seat and he drifted off to sleep, head heavy on his neck.

The next thing he remembers with any certainty is waking up in a hospital bed, desperately thirsty and incredibly tired. Catching his uncle's face in the chair next to his bed. Hans knew immediately that some piece was out of place, but he struggled to put it all together. Uncle Thomas looked as though he'd been there for a while. His skin was greasy, his face stippled with the beginnings of a beard, dark pools under his eyes. As Hans struggled to sit up, his uncle jerked out of his reverie, reached for the boy's hands. That squeeze communicated more to Hans than the words that followed. He understood that his parents were dead. That they'd entrusted him to his uncle as guardian, should anything ever happen to them. The scratches on his small face stung with the salt of his tears.

It was the last time he would cry for many years. He stayed in the hospital for a week, and in that time, he managed to entomb his emotions behind an impermeable façade. Thomas took him in, and he was launched into a prosperous family with high expectations. His cousins seemed to thrive under that pressure. Music lessons, sports, drama, art classes, riding lessons – they excelled at almost everything, and when they didn't, they quickly dropped the offending activity for something new. His uncle expected Hans to do the same. The boy did his best, but he had to work harder than the others. He ran well enough, he acted passably in school productions. He got up early every morning to iron his shirts until the creases were perfectly bladed. But he never won any races, never got the leading role. Eventually he discovered that while his natural limitations kept him from reaching the highest levels in extracurriculars, he could excel in his studies. So he worked hard to get the highest marks. He studied until he had no more time for friends or social activities.

Hans' grandmother was the anchor of the family, although he never met her until after the accident. When he was a baby, his mother took him with her when she left her first marriage and ran off with a wealthy man. He was raised in luxury, as an only child. He had met his uncle once, when he and his oldest son came to visit, but the rest of his cousins and his grandmother had remained shadows behind glass. He never saw photos, and his mother never told stories about them.

Meeting his grandmother defined the course of his future. She had escaped from the Nazis during the Second World War, fled east, and returned to Germany after the war with nothing. She had worked hard to claw back something of what she'd lost, but she was never rich, never secure. She pushed all of her grandchildren to achieve, to follow the strict protocols of German high society, to belong in that world, because she thought this would finally cement their security as a family. In a way, Hans' mother had inherited this insecurity. When she ran away, it was to marry a man from that world, to escape her middle-class life and build something stronger, more stable, for herself and for her son. But all of that was undone in a moment.

Hans' grandmother was always sure of herself in every situation, calm and strong. She never raised her voice, but her anger was legendary. She would hold grudges until the offender came bowing and scraping with apologies, but then she would always forgive warmly and whole-heartedly. She kept them all unbalanced, granting and withholding approval strategically until she pushed them onto the path she thought was best. She chose the medical profession for Hans, perhaps because his step-father had been a doctor, and even while she hated her daughter for running away, she admired the world she'd fled into. She wanted that for her grandson, and for herself. She always encouraged Hans to work as hard as he could, to push himself to the outer edges of his limits. He spent countless hours after school scouring medical texts. He planned to become a surgeon. And he did his best to live up to her expectations.

But in the end, he would never perform surgery. The first time he had to assist in an operating theater, he froze. The body on the cold steel table petrified him completely. What if he made a mistake? What if something he did cost this person, so still and trusting on the table, her life? He kept imagining his mother's body, lifeless under a damp white sheet by the roadside. His hands shook so much that he couldn't go through with it. Furious with himself, he tried again the next week. And again. The result was always the same. He could never be a perfect surgeon, because such a thing didn't exist. Death was an inevitable part of the profession. He was paralyzed. He labored under the knowledge that he'd disappointed his grandmother, wasted his uncle's money on an education he couldn't use. He'd let his family down. He'd failed.

On some level, all he'd ever really wanted was a relaxed, easygoing life. His fear was a way of protecting himself from the hard work and long hours that inevitably go into practicing medicine. When it became clear that he'd never be a surgeon, he went into research instead, working for a biotechnology firm, developing medicines and traveling to conferences. It was a comparatively relaxed world, and it gave him the chance to travel and meet different people in various fields. He learned a lot, and was more or less content. But he always felt the weight of his family's disappointment. Piled on top of that, the weight of his failed marriage was almost too much for him to bear. Marrying Kerstin had been his greatest success in his grandmother's eyes. For the first few months after the divorce, he often felt as if he was being held underwater by a pressure that no amount of effort could lift from his shoulders.

Hana did her best to set him free from all that. Her own imperfections, in her childhood, in her past relationships, in her physical appearance, had freed her from the straitjacket of perfectionism. With Hana, he reminisced about childhood, the effect their different experiences had on each of them as adults. These histories cast harsh shadows of difference when it came to their early years. Although the chaos in Hana's childhood was very real, she did her best to purge it from her system. She wanted to be able to live differently. Eventually she learned to navigate the world on her own, but she never healed completely. The scars went too deep. As she grew into adulthood, mindful of her own needs as well as those of others, she took matters into her own hands. She made sure she was never a burden to anyone.

Hana firmly believed that craving should be contained, resisted. Any kind of hunger, whether emotional or physical, had destructive potential. She said that the way to wisdom was appreciating what was available, and never complaining that it wasn't enough. Hana was deeply enamored with Hans, but she was also open about her concerns. About their geographical distance, the cultural barriers, family structures, and most of all, the fact that he was fifteen years younger. Hans didn't worry about differences. He knew Hana was exactly what he needed.

But life is full of paradoxes and enigmas. No one knows how their story will end. Hana was a natural nurturer, and more than anything, Hans wanted to seal their bond with marriage. To him, this was the perfect, the only ending. On the surface, their relationship already seemed perfect. But there was one undercurrent of imperfection even Hans could not control.

In the beginning, Hans expected Hana to still his every craving. She filled him up. She was his guru. He felt he belonged to her. He joked about their similar names. The fact that it seemed too good to be true was to him proof that it was meant to be. He believed in soulmates, and he believed Hana was his.

He learned to eat spicy food so he could enjoy the full range of her cooking. He tried to make love to her every day. He wanted nothing more than to please her, to impress her, to impress on other people the strength of their bond, the fact that they belonged together. He bought shirts, pants, and socks in every color of the rainbow so he could match her aesthetic, her style. So people would notice them together. Hana was a dot of color in a city where nearly everyone wore black. She was a trendsetter. Hans made a joke of it.

"Look, I'm your first follower!"

She gazed steadily at him, but didn't laugh.

In their first years together, he was full of ideas. He quit his job in medical research and made plans to start a think tank, where he could be the CEO. He bought books about holistic medicine and thought about going back to school, opening his own practice. When none of his plans bore fruit, he joined volunteer organizations, sports clubs. He surrounded himself with the kind of alpha males he wanted to emulate.

All the rules he'd been following since childhood suddenly seemed stuffy and tight. He found freedom with Hana in Berlin. He saw a glittering future in which he could be completely open, with the world and with her. She would be his gateway to success.

For Hans, Hana was a Madonna, the perfect image of a mother. Nurturing, caring, confident, secure. Everything a child needs. And he wanted her to have his children. He wanted dozens of them. He suggested IVF, but she laughed it off. As time went on, he gave up on that plan. But he wanted her to get to know his children. He wanted them to be her children, too.

Hans had accepted Kerstin's desire for custody of their kids without resisting. It was what she wanted, what she said was best. And it gave him the chance to pursue something new. Soon after Hana arrived in Berlin, she started looking for an apartment of her own. She wanted to live separately, to have her own space for painting and creative work. And she wanted Hans to have his own apartment, with his children. He panicked. All he wanted was Hana, and he felt she was already holding him at arm's length.

He was swept up in their love. He cancelled his lease without telling her, and then insisted on moving in with her. For the first few months, he stopped going to visit his children on weekends. Then they started coming to Berlin on the train to see him. As he watched them spend time with Hana, he convinced himself they could be the perfect family. He began inviting them to come more often. At first, Kerstin was reluctant, but in the end, the free weekends left her with more time to pursue her own interests, which was what she'd wanted at the end of their marriage. Hana was pleased to have them around. Together she and Hans took the children to museums, to the pool. She bought them presents. Hans believed she had started to think of herself as their mother, just as he had.

One night over dinner, carried away by the warm glow of the wine and his giddy visions of the future, he sprang a question on the table.

"How would you like to move in with us?"

Hana put down her fork as if it had suddenly gained ten pounds. All three children turned to him in surprise.

"We could do up the spare bedroom for you. And Hana's studio could be a second bedroom. You'd have to share." He finished the wine in his glass. "But think how wonderful it would be to live in Berlin! All of us together!"

The children sat up straight, looked around at each other, at Hana. But when Hans met her eyes across the table, she shook her head, just the tiniest fraction. She didn't say a word for the rest of the meal.

Later that night, after the children were in bed, Hans confronted Hana.

"Why didn't you make any effort at dinner?" He was angry. "How could you be so quiet when they were so enthusiastic?"

"They weren't enthusiastic, Hans. They were nervous."

"That's because you were discouraging them!" He threw his hands into the air. "How are we going to be a family if you won't act like their mother?"

She looked at him for a long moment, and finally spoke so quietly that he had to ask her to repeat herself.

"I've already done that."

"What do you mean? This would just be the next step."

She explained slowly, as if just coming to the realization herself.

"No, I mean that I've already had that time in my life. Your children have a mother. They need her. I'm happy to spend time with them, to have them here with us. But I am not their mother. They don't need me. They need to live with their father."

"But I need you! I need us to be a family."

She was shaking her head.

"But you're a caretaker! That's your gift. This way, you can take care of all of us."

The look she gave him then was the beginning of the end.

Over the years they were together, people often unthinkingly referred to Hana as Hans' wife. He did what he could to encourage that perception. But she was not his wife, and the word just rubbed more salt into an open wound.

For years, he had wanted Hana to become his wife. He'd proposed marriage to her a dozen times. He wanted her with him wherever he went. He wanted her to accompany him on every trip, every conference. He wanted her next to him at every meal. He saw this as proof of the depth and breadth of his love. The desire never to be apart, not for a moment. More than anything, he had wanted their love for each other cemented in ink and ceremony, so that she could never be wrenched away from him. But Hana had ridden the storms of two difficult marriages, and by the time she and Hans found each other, she was determined never to legally bind herself to anyone else. And she never budged, no matter what he said. It became the only subject he couldn't risk bringing up with her.

Hana wanted peace, the calm contentment that comes with experience, with honest self-reflection. Hans believed that marriage would provide that. Security, stability. But she saw it differently. He demanded reasons. She talked about independence, about her distaste for traditional relationship models. They argued, and the calm that used to encompass them in the morning was swept away in a stony silence. She did not want to marry him, and that was that. It was a staggering blow for Hans, to be told over and over again by the woman he'd come to love most in the world, to need most, that she was not willing to tie her future to him legally. It reminded him of Kerstin's rejection. It reignited the spark of insecurity he thought he'd finally escaped.

On their final day, Hana bustles around Hans while he struggles with the tension in the air. He sits silently at the long wooden dining table, tracing its worn surface, drifting back to all the dinner parties they've hosted together over the course of their relationship. All the fun they've had. The coffee maker buzzes and jitters. She sets two cappuccinos down on the table, slides into the chair across from him. He lurches the cup out of his way, foam sloshing over the rim and into the saucer. He reaches across to her.

"Marry me." It is not a question. She drops her eyes to her coffee and slowly shakes her head.

"You know I can't live without you. I need you so much." Everything he has become is wrapped up in her. She is the skin holding him together.

"Hans, you already know my answer. Why do you keep asking me?"

He tries to tighten his grip as she disentangles her hand. Without a word, she gets up, takes a cup in each hand, and goes to the kitchen to pour the tepid coffee into the sink.

They pass the morning in complete silence, until she comes and puts a hand on his shoulder to ask if he'd like to join her for lunch. They cross the street like strangers and make their way to the cheap but cheerful café where they'd spent so many laughing lunches. They order the special, something they've eaten countless times before – fresh grilled herring sandwiches with onions and pickles. A Berlin delicacy.

Hans swallows the herring in three quick bites. He barely pauses to appreciate it. The saltiness of the fish, the sting of the onion, forgotten the next second. Hana never eats this way. She always tastes everything, patiently, deliberately. He's stuck, the food knotted in his stomach, waiting for each of her slow, thoughtful bites. He aches to hold her hand as he waits. But she has both hands on her sandwich, gazing through the plate glass window at the small park across the street, its fountain dry and packed with fallen leaves. He has to content himself with an awkward hold on her arm. An unwelcome reminder that he can't force her into the shape he wants her to fill.

In that moment, he knows it's really over. He's given Hana one last chance. He needs a woman who will support him, who will step into the role of mother for his children. And he's already come up with another plan.

Chapter 8:
Karma's Gameplay

Fate always
stands by destiny
ready
to invite occasion.

Singing,
What must be, must be.

The fatalist's fetish,
consequences
of Karma's gameplay.

As long as
no god
elects a certain soul,
we gladly receive.

Singing,
What must be, must be.

Berlin is a place of new hope and forgiveness. It is a place of struggle and creation. We were no different from anyone else who went there seeking a fresh start. Berlin still holds the melancholy, the pain and suffering of the past, and we let it intermingle with our daily routines. Berlin always felt like the right place for healing.

Hans was an essential part of my healing, too. Being

with such a charming, funny, loving man in such an open, creative city was something I could never have imagined for myself. We met by chance, at the home of a German art collector. The medical research center of which Christian von Bergstein was a trustee had given considerable funding to Roger, and they had become friends. After my divorce, Roger had connected me with Christian. He was a patron of the arts, interested in building a museum in the small town where his family spent their summers. He loved spotting new talent, nurturing artists with time and space to create. He was fascinated with my art and commissioned me to do a series of large paintings for his collection. That project helped support me at a difficult time. It gave me something to do, somewhere to go. He invited me to visit Germany, to stay at his family's summer home in Lübeck as a kind of artist-in-residence.

While I was there, I got a message from Hélie. After a long silence, I received an email telling me that his wife had passed away six months before. He said he was processing his grief. I wrote back immediately, told him I was very sorry for his loss. I thought I might visit him in Paris at the end of the summer, but I didn't tell him about my plan. I was still considering the best course of action when fate intervened once again.

Hans was open, sympathetic, humanitarian. The night we met felt like a magical confluence of souls, an intense conversation about everything life had thrown at us, and how we had survived. In those weeks together, our days were full of laughter and hope. We talked about moving forward, about what we both wanted from life. I thought of my idol, Salomé, and her relationship with Rilke, who was much younger. How much they had enjoyed each other over the years. How they had pushed each other to new heights of creativity. I wondered whether, at sixty, I could modernize myself yet again.

After the long absence of physical intimacy in my marriage to Sam, I was determined to have fun. My children encouraged me to take every opportunity to enjoy myself while I was in Germany. My friends told me to enjoy it while it lasted. I took their advice and threw myself into what I thought was a lighthearted, carefree relationship.

After that first summer in Berlin, I came back to San Francisco, to my children and my friends. Hans went off to Brazil to fulfill his dream of working with Doctors Without Borders. At that time, I had no expectations. There were many paths open to me. But still, I hesitated over responding to Hélie's message. Finally I sent him a poem I'd written, called "The Weight of Love." I felt that each of the different loves in my life had a different heft, different gravity. Hans was spontaneous, fun. I thought we would enjoy each other for a time. The feeling I had for Hélie was something else, something deeper. A longing for a mystery man, someone I hardly knew, and yet felt I understood. That feeling made me cautious. I was not prepared to be hurt again. And after so much time spent caring for others, I needed time to discover how best to care for myself.

Hélie wrote back almost immediately. He told me it was the first time he'd ever received a poem. He understood my sentiments perfectly. It was the first time he called me "my love." I sat with those words, debating with myself how to respond. In the end, I didn't.

When Hans returned to Berlin after only a month, I didn't know what to think. On one hand, he was charming and handsome, well-educated and funny. So gentle, so loving, so persistent in his affection for me. And Berlin offered the chance for a new start, a place full of energy and inspiration. Just what I needed in those days. But the way he described his lovesickness, the way he had given up a lifelong dream to rush back to my arms, made me hesitate. Did I have the strength to sustain that kind of intense connection over the long term? Could I uproot my life again without knowing where all this was leading?

My friends and family saw me enjoying myself and thought I should make the most of it. My friends told me I was lucky to have such a young, handsome man in my life. My children saw his adoration for me, so different from their father, and they thought I deserved to experience that kind of love. Even Roger, who expressed his reservations about Hans, told me that he had never seen me so positive and peaceful. I felt like I had mastered the art of happiness, of enjoying myself while maintaining a certain sense of detachment. And I thought Hans was one reason why.

So I went to Berlin. It was electric. The human condition is everywhere – out on the street, out in the open.

Berlin's history has molded the city into a poignant, eye-opening display of the amount of pain humanity can inflict and endure, and yet that is precisely the source of its creativity. It bears its scars proudly. Berlin still has unfinished business, and the space it creates provides people looking for alternative lifestyles and opportunities with the possibilities that are lacking almost everywhere else. No one needs to fit the mold in Berlin. There is a vast heartbeat, one you can feel on the street as people flit in and out of bars and restaurants, as music pulses from clubs, as art is spray-painted onto walls, as people from all over the world come and discover new ways of living together. The city gave me back my life, and it bound Hans and me together.

Our first years together were full of warmth and light. We threw dinner parties for friends he'd known for years, for people we met at gallery openings and the symphony. I filled my home with laughter, color, and food. I set about making my space into one inhabited and enlivened by hope, the hope we'd each given back to each other. I was content with him. I felt I could truly be myself, and he would love me for who I was.

It was an incredibly creative period for me. I was truly happy. I had no attachments pulling me down. I felt free. And his devotion, his constant assurances of love and affection, were just what I had been missing for so many years. But that kind of devotion can also turn into something darker. An unhealthy obsession.

It began with his plans for us to move in together.

The apartment he had rented was too small for both of us, and once my paintings arrived, it became clear that there was no space for me to do creative work. I found another place, an apartment filled with light, with floor-to-ceiling windows overlooking a park. In that park stood a beautiful neoclassical church that had been bombed during the Second World War, restored over long decades and transformed into a cultural center. It was a powerful place, and although I am not religious, I still believe in spiritual energy. Every morning and evening, when I sat down at the dining table, I watched the clouds forming and disintegrating in the sky, the changing light playing off the warm golden façade. It seemed like the perfect place to for me to dream. That neighborhood was the most vibrant, bohemian, wild place in the world. Surrounded by the life of the city, the vast beating heart of Berlin, I took all that light and energy to my studio. I painted every day.

Hans and I were spending every evening together, and he often stayed the night. Slowly, the new, bright clothes he bought found their way into my closet, and his collections of shoes and ties and sports equipment began to fill up my drawers and shelves. In a way, he had already moved in even before we talked about it seriously.

One morning over breakfast, he told me that he was planning to give up his lease at the end of the month. I was surprised.

"What about your kids?"

I hadn't been counting the weekends, but I knew that

he'd been spending all of his spare time with me, and it seemed like quite a while since he'd been to visit them.

"Maybe you should think about finding an apartment with rooms for them. A separate place just for you. Somewhere they could come and stay."

"I don't think their mother would allow it." He always referred to his ex-wife this way, never by her name.

"How do you know? They need their father. If you had space for them—"

"We have plenty of space here. They can visit us here."

"It's not the same, Hans. They need a place to be with their father."

That was the first time I saw him sulk. It became a pattern in our relationship. We would disagree, he would fall into a depression, and I would give in. Even then, I knew it was the same pattern I'd pinned myself to all my life. The nurturer, the enabler, the caretaker. The one who gives of herself until she has nothing left for herself. But even so, I gave in. He cancelled his lease and moved in with me. In those early days, he was often euphoric. We started spending every waking moment together.

He filled the apartment with his collections. Matchboxes and business cards scattered across every flat surface. Mementos of places we'd been together, people we'd met. He left these tokens where they could be seen whenever anyone came to visit. Whenever he met anyone, he'd ask endless questions until he found some connection to his own history, however tenuous. He idolized his colleagues when he agreed with them, and put them down viciously when he didn't. He claimed deep friendships with people he'd barely met. His emotional highs and lows were steep and extreme. But I learned to ride the rollercoaster. I was experienced.

I learned to judge his moods by his posture. When he was down, he'd walk the streets like a penguin, toes turned out, head down, shuffling. He would come home with coins he'd found on the sidewalk, in the gutter, because he was looking down at his own feet everywhere he went. He kept this coin collection in a metal box under our bed. But when he was on one of his emotional highs, he would charge into the closet in the morning, asking what I was planning to wear so that he could select complementary colors for himself. He declared his readiness to die for me. He talked nonstop. I'd never had this kind of love, the kind of obsessive, urgent need most people experience in their teenage years. My childhood circumstances had denied me all that. And here it was. But I was not a teenage girl any more. What he jokingly referred to as his love bombs began to stifle me. But if I ever showed my frustration, he would spiral deep into a black hole, and it would be up to me to pull him out. When I tried to disentangle myself, to pull away even a little bit, to create some air and space where I could breathe, he clung on even tighter.

He wanted to have sex every day. He saw it as another way to cement our connection, to ensure I stayed close to him.

"It's ridiculous," I laughed. "No one can have that much sex. It's impossible."

But that didn't stop him from trying. At the beginning, I sometimes felt like he wanted to eat me alive. My creative energy dwindled.

But it would be years before I finally decided that I couldn't spend my life taking care of other people. That it was time to take care of myself.

As our relationship entered the more sedate stage after the first flush of love, Hans began to talk more about his children. But still he neglected them. He didn't want to leave me to visit them, and I didn't think it was a good idea for me to go along. But they found ways to get his attention. Once he moved in, they started calling at all hours, day and night. After a nightmare, his son would pick up the phone. Hans would answer the phone next to the bed, and then roll over and hand it to me. And his son would hang up. Hans thought we needed to be one big, happy family. I thought his son needed his father.

It was me who suggested they should come to stay with us on the weekends. I thought I was doing the best thing, for him and for them. I truly enjoyed spending time with them. But gradually, whenever they came, Hans bowed out. He expected me to take care of them constantly. If there was anything they needed, it was up to me to provide it. That's what he thought a mother's love should be. Providing the kind of security he'd never had. I had managed to build an emotional home for my children without ever having such a home myself. And I wondered what it was that prevented Hans from doing the same. But I was not prepared to reinsert myself into this maternal role.

As Hans told me more about his own childhood, I began to understand. The instability he'd faced, losing his parents at such a young age, and the pressure to achieve, to climb the social ladder, had all left a lasting mark on him. More than anything, he needed to belong. He needed to be perfect. I tried to provide him with the assurance that he would always belong to me. I gave of myself continually, but his insecurity was ravenous. I could never fill him up, no matter how much of me he gobbled down.

For most of our relationship, I thought it was my turn to be the savior. I was the mature one, the one who had seen so much of life's ups and downs. I had come full circle since Brian, who had tried to save me, and Sam, who had held me down and pushed me away. Now I was in the position of power. It was gratifying, at first. But Hans' financial and emotional dependence wore me down. As I became his mother figure, he became increasingly juvenile. Where I had worked hard to break the cycle of negativity and rejection, to shatter the structures I'd been brought up in and build something else for myself and my children, Hans was still trapped in the straightjacket of perfectionism. And as hard as I tried, I could not free him.

When one of his colleagues at the research center was promoted to a position ahead of him, he began to have anxiety attacks. He had trouble breathing in the morning before he left for work. The single glass of wine he used to drink each night became two, then three. He gained weight, his masculine features filled out into something round and boyish. He developed a twitch in the muscle around his eye. He lost his voice for weeks at a time. Finally, one night, he came home and announced he'd quit his job. He simply couldn't stand working for that person another minute.

It was another spectacular high that didn't last. He wanted to try something new. He expected success to come easy. He always felt he deserved more. He wanted someone to support his heady plans. He decided to give up his medical education and found a think tank. He was full of ideas, but he never had the energy to accompany them into reality. I wondered where all the effort had gone, this little boy who had studied medical textbooks after school. Who had wanted to volunteer in the most dire circumstances to help treat people in need. As he started reaching for the free and easy life he'd never had as a child, I saw all that energy poured into one cup after another – a few drops in each, and then he moved on to the next. He was flailing. He wanted the stimulation that comes with the new, but it was only in rituals and routines that he found any security. When he knew how to behave, what to expect. When he could be perfect. New things attracted him with the promise of finally finding the one great talent that would come naturally to him, but the insecurity of it all left him terrified.

I don't blame him. We're all warped by the damage we've sustained in life. It's not a matter of fault. It's simply that living in the world involves creating pain as well as bearing it. We are all scarred by our suffering. I believed in unconditional love, and I wanted to give it. I didn't have the heart to kick him out. I knew he had no means to survive without me.

I hoped he would develop. I expected him to find his feet again, to stop dangling his weight off of me and find his place in the world, the place where he could belong, where he could excel, where he could relax. With my help, I thought he would discover it. That we would search it out together. I thought he would be strong enough to develop his own life with his children. That we could live together but apart, with some distance between us, where we would each find space for ourselves. My creative vision was filling my head and pushing up against the backs of my eyes, desperate to find an outlet. But whenever I took the time I needed to paint or to write, Hans would come knocking on the door of my studio with questions, cups of tea, restaurant reservations with friends. For him, that was love. But I was suffocating.

When he started hiding from me, I knew it was over. When he stopped coming into the closet in the morning to find out what I was wearing. When he stayed home while I went out. When he stopped asking his children to come for the weekend. When he came home every day weighed down by the coins he picked up. What I didn't know was that he'd already made his escape plan.

Hans believed in soulmates. That fusion of souls that will redeem each of us and banish loneliness, if only we can find the right person. He believed in sex as the ultimate expression of love, and he needed it for reassurance. He wanted safety and excitement, and he refused to come to terms with the fact that it's nearly impossible to achieve both of those things in one relationship. He believed that the perfect romance was waiting somewhere out there. When it turned out that our relationship was not perfect, that I would never fill the mold he had in his mind, he began looking for that perfect partner again. The one who would finally fill his void.

What he found was a Sicilian woman he met online. Ever since I'd known him, he'd been obsessed with the Godfather. Films about filial devotion, about forgiveness, about unconditional acceptance within a tightknit family. He watched those movies over and over again, religiously. In the time we lived together, he wore out three separate DVDs. So when I rejected what turned out to be his final marriage proposal, he went in search of that particular dream. The ready-made fallback family.

Hans had proposed marriage more times than I could count. He needed that financial security, that official piece of paper, that ritual and ceremony to bind us together. But I had long ago decided never to tie myself to another man in that way. I thought our relationship could go on as it was, that we would find a better balance as partners than as man and wife. But marriage was another club that Hans wanted to be a member of. And I underestimated just how badly he wanted to belong.

On our last day together, he didn't ask me to marry him so much as he demanded it. He presented it as an ultimatum. Marry him or else it was over. I sat across from him at the table where we'd hosted so many dinner parties, stunned. Once again, I described all the reasons why I couldn't marry him. How long I'd struggled to find my balance on own two feet. The resilience it had taken to break out of my old patterns and find a new way of being in the world. The space I needed for my creative work. And the fact that I couldn't take on the responsibility of being a mother to his children. I'd passed that time in my life. I could not take that step. I could not commit myself to him in that way. And I could not understand why he would not stop asking for what I could not give.

The next morning, I had a warm bath and went out alone in search of inspiration for a new painting I was working on. Our daily rituals had long since fallen into irregularity, so I was not surprised when he didn't want to accompany me to the baker for our usual morning croissants. I walked for hours, admiring the fall colors and the golden autumn light flooding the streets. I breathed deep and felt free. And when I got home, he wasn't there.

There was a note on the dining room table. He'd written a few short sentences. Telling me that he couldn't stay with someone who didn't want to commit to him. That he had to do what was best for his children. That he'd taken just a backpack, and he wouldn't be back. Three sentences put an end to our seven years together.

I checked the closet. Most of his clothes were still there. I checked under the bed. The metal box of coins he'd brought back from so many solitary, depressed walks was gone.

Over the next few days, I painted almost without a break. From morning to night, without eating and almost without drinking, I covered canvases with the emotion that came pouring out of me. Exhilaration, a rush of delight in the silence and space around me. After nearly a week, I stood back from my work, and what I saw was myself. As if in a magical mirror, all the thoughts that couldn't be put into words were spread across the canvas in startling brightness. I thought I'd done some of my best work yet.

Two days later, Hans' daughter called. She was in tears, inconsolable. It took me some time to piece her words together into sense. Hans had found someone else. He was planning to marry her the very next weekend. He wanted his children to be there.

"How could he do this to you?"

I tried to soothe her. I took the phone into my studio and sat on the floor, staring at my paintings while we talked.

"Don't worry about me. I will be fine. I am fine."

She couldn't understand her father. I tried to explain. To give her some context in which to put his actions. To help her find generous explanations for his behavior. To help her feel what he was feeling.

"But I love you! I don't want to lose you!"

"You won't. You are always welcome in my home, in my life. You have a place here. Unconditionally."

When she was calm, we hung up. And I felt a wave of relief. As if my glass-walled studio had become an aquarium, and I was submerged.

When I finally got up, it was dark. I went around the apartment, turning on every light. I collected all the things he'd left behind, the things that wouldn't fit into his backpack – Hermes ties, designer shoes, expensive cufflinks. I piled it all in his home office and shut the door.

He never came back for his things. I never heard another word from him.

Through my seven years in Berlin, Hélie was always in the back of my mind. The perfect fantasy romance. But it could only be perfect because it remained unfulfilled. I was not ready for another commitment. I was not prepared to risk what I'd just barely begun to regain. He continued to email me periodically. Out of loyalty to Hans, I had stopped responding to him. But that longing was always there. Hélie was worried because he hadn't heard from me. He couldn't reach me by phone. He hoped I was well, that I was happy.

Another of these messages arrived a few months after

Hans left. I sent a reply, telling him I was in Berlin. That I was alone, but not lonely. I told him about the latest crossroads where I found myself standing, staring down the different paths open before me. A global citizen with a bohemian spirit, I thought I could go anywhere. But I couldn't stay where I was. I felt stranded in Berlin, hemmed in by memories.

His reply came within the hour. He suggested I come to Paris for a visit. It had been so long since we'd seen each other. And the final line of his email tugged at my heart.

"I'm still longing for you."

I responded simply. "Me too."

I was ready for a change. A trip to Paris seemed like just the thing to draw me out of myself. I agreed to come that very weekend.

As the plane circled Charles de Gaulle airport, I felt again the sense of loss I'd first felt on that long-ago flight from Korea. Of having left some part of myself behind, of descending into the unknown. I wondered what I would find when I landed. Would I even recognize him? It had been eighteen years since we'd seen each other. Would the spark we felt that night so long ago still be there? Or would we simply be old friends, happy to catch up, and just as happy to go our separate ways afterwards?

As I exited the terminal, a uniformed driver stood in front of a black sedan, holding up a sign with my name on it. My French was rusty, but I understood that he would take me to my hotel, and Hélie would meet me there once I'd had a chance to settle in.

In my hotel room, I found three dozen pink roses and a card, signed with just his name. My eyes filled with tears, but I blinked them away. I wanted to see him first, before I let the emotion wash over me. When the call came from the front desk a few minutes later, I found my hand shaking as I replaced the receiver.

Downstairs in the lobby, amid the red velvet couches and fresh flowers, sat the very man I remembered. His face had aged, webbed with new lines I didn't recognize. But then, so had mine. He lit up as I stepped out of the elevator. He took my arm, leaned in to kiss both of my cheeks, with all that had passed between us over the years hovering in the air around us.

"I made a reservation at the Plaza Athénée. Unless there's somewhere else you'd like to go, my love?"

I gripped his soft fingers.

"Can you take me to the place where we met?"

He took me to the same restaurant, ordered the same coq au vin. And we talked about all the years that had come in between. He smiled across the table at me.

"I emailed Pierre to tell him we were meeting, after all this time."

The waiters still knew him by name, and he was still the perfect gentleman, treating everyone with respectful attention. He asked me questions about my life in Berlin, and he listened to my answers with the same careful consideration I gave him. Once again, we talked until everyone else was gone and our candle was the last one burning.

The next morning, I took myself out for a walk. The

wind was cold, but the streets of Paris were warm with memories. The air in the parks smelled like the first green flush of spring, and there were crocuses poking up through the tired, wilted grass. I was flooded with emotion. For years, I had pushed the waves of my grief firmly back behind an impermeable breakwater. The grief of my childhood, the grief of Brian's disappearance, the grief at the end of my marriage to Sam, and the grief of Hans' departure. I had had moments of uncontrollable emotion, which I usually channeled into painting or poetry. But it wasn't until that morning in Paris that I was able to let it wash over me. The feeling had piled up so high behind that carefully constructed breakwater that the release of seeing Hélie was enough to cause the final surge.

It came all at once, unexpectedly, as I was sitting at a sidewalk café enjoying the thin winter sunshine. A little girl toddled by, her tiny mittened hand clutched in her father's glove, and she stopped to stare at me. Her father tried to coax her on, but she held eye contact with me for several moments, the way small children will, with no sense of embarrassment. When she finally broke that gaze, I found tears streaming down my face, and then I was weeping. It took many minutes for me to compose myself enough to walk back to the hotel.

Once I got there, I let it all pour out. I hadn't realized just how much grief there was. Grief for myself, for the little girl I'd been and the pain I'd endured. Grief for my father, who never knew what it was to love. Grief for Brian, who might be dead or alive. Grief for Sam, who had lost everything before he'd realized that he'd had it. Grief for Hans, who so desperately needed something that he would most likely never find. And grief for the time I'd wasted doing everyone else's bidding. For the long years it had taken me to find the strength I needed to break out of those old patterns. To become, not who I wanted to be, but who I actually was.

When I finally got up and went to splash cold water on my face, I looked steadily into the mirror. I saw the face I'd gone through nearly seventy years of life with, as if for the first time. Red and swollen from crying, imperfect by any standard, and yet mine. With all my pain and all my joy written there for the world to read. And although I could not smile, I was overwhelmed with gratitude.

I texted Hélie the word he'd asked me for all those years ago. Resilience. Just a single word to express so much. Thirty minutes later, he knocked on my door. Slowly, gently, we consummated the love we'd been carrying for each other through so many years. The human feeling of it overwhelmed us both. I couldn't think of those years as wasted, because they had shaped us both into the people we were, there in that room. The love I felt was more than attraction, more than simple affection. It was much deeper, much more complex. This was yet another kind of love, a deep, still well of empathy and compassion. Our images of each other were pure, not sullied by experience. We had nothing to hide, and no need for defense. It had taken me sixty-eight years to get here, but finally, here I was.

I returned to Berlin. Alone, but content, and no longer suffering. I am finally finding the balance between caring for others and caring for myself.

Hélie, as I always expected, is the consummate gentleman. He knows how to treat an independent woman. He understands what I need. He expects me to make my own decisions, and he does not expect to be at the center of them. He tells me he is there waiting whenever I want to see him. He still longs for me. He still calls me "my love." He wants me to live my life, and to share what I can of it with him. We want to enjoy each other and whatever time we have left together. We are both free. Ready for a new adventure.

Once, after spending the afternoon at the Musée d'Orsay, I wandered across the street to visit the National Museum of the Legion of Honor and the Orders of Chivalry. I knew that Roger had been awarded such an honor after his Nobel Prize, and I wanted to pay my respects. I was alone in the museum, and I struck up a conversation with the guard.

"Does Madame know someone who is honored in this museum?"

I gave him Roger's name, and he led me to the appropriate case, embossed in gold and lit with warm light. The sight of my mentor's name brought tears to my eyes. The guard stood back for a moment, then approached with another question.

"Does Madame know anyone else in France? Perhaps there is another name."

I told him that I had come to Paris to visit an old friend. And I gave him Hélie's name. To my surprise, he led me to another case. There, etched on a deep red velvet background, was a medal confirming Hélie's induction as a Chevalier of the Ordre national du Mérite.

"This family is old French nobility," the guard explained. "Your friend is famous."

"But he never told me!" I exclaimed as I traced my finger over the glass. He smiled.

"Madame, a true gentleman never tells."

Hélie continued to surprise me. Sam had taken me to a litany of famous French restaurants on our travels. But Hélie's choices were more to my taste. Food like a piece of abstract art on a plate, served by impeccable waiters in elegant rooms. When I remarked on how well his choices suited me, he smiled, held out his palms.

"You deserve to have the best. I want to take you to places that are inspired. Refined. Original." His smile widened. "Like you."

The dishes reminded me of my own paintings, as if my art and my cooking had been combined just for me. The flavors were mysterious, delicious, and deeply pleasurable. Our evenings together were full of surprise and delight. Hélie understood that my lifelong fascination with food is part of my creative spirit. He wanted nothing more than to please me. And I felt I had finally learned how to accept all the pleasures life offered.

I was in Paris on Roger's ninety-sixth birthday. I called to wish him well, as I always did, no matter where I was in the world. His wife Lucianne answered the phone, told me that he was in the hospital. He was set to undergo brain surgery after an aneurism. He was in good spirits, as ever. Lucianne told me not to worry. But I knew the seriousness of the situation. And I knew I needed to see him again.

So here I am, in yet another airport, waiting to cross yet another ocean. For love, once again. It's the story of my life. And I am intensely grateful.

Chapter 9:
Weights and Measures

The heart speaks
volumes
that cannot be imprinted.
We manage unexpected expectation.

You gave me wings to fly,
and I touched down in your heart.
Even love's weight is heavy.
But this feels like my home.

You showered me with your best,
I ignored my worst.
You became my thirst,
I became your hunger.
In winter, the fire burns brightest.

We eat together in a winter garden
devoid of green.
We accept life whole,
not in halves.
We break the glass,
then the rules,
then the mold.

Free
to give
to love
to long
for even more.

How could I have anticipated returning to Korea fifty years later? My returns up till now have been sporadic, my feelings about the culture I grew up in ambivalent. How could they be anything else? I call myself a global citizen. Sometimes it's a lonely freedom to inhabit. But it is my choice.

Pressure turns stone to diamonds, as long as you don't disintegrate to powder. As the plane touches down in Seoul, I think of my old red-banded Japanese watch, long given up its ghosts. And I smile.

Today is my seventieth birthday. Much has changed since the day I entered the world, and much has stayed the same. Korea is still divided, but the possibility of reunification looms large on the horizon. My life is a microcosm of these fragile hopes. The uncertainty of circumstances, the vulnerability inherent in trusting other people, the difficulty of forgiveness, faith and the lack of it.

I've come back for my sister's funeral. David and Mia sit beside me on the plane, squeezed into a narrow row of three cramped seats. They laugh when I tell them about the PanAm flight I took all those years ago, the enormous plush chairs, the businessmen smoking on the plane. This time, I've brought only a small suitcase. Detachment is something I learned in the temple, balanced on the precipice between my old life and my new one. I'm relearning it now, at the end of my life. Disentangling myself from objects, from dependence.

My nephew meets us outside baggage claim. The sight

of his face releases a tide of emotion. Anxiety, fear, and grief wash out of me through my tears. I spend my days with family. With my nephew and my nieces, with their children. With my cousins, and their children, and their grandchildren. David and Mia meet some of their cousins for the first time. The conversation weaves a tapestry of English and Korean. The sounds of their voices, echoes of my sister, bring more tears. But these are tears of joy. Moments of ecstasy that borders on religious. This is proof of my sister's strength, her creativity. This beautiful new generation of my family. My hope for the future. My resolution.

My cousins tell stories of lingering pain. Of my father wrenching my arm until I cried out. Of my stepmother chasing me with a big stick. Of the 1960 typhoon that nearly drowned us all. Of the ones who stayed behind. I can't bring myself to return to the town I grew up in. I still have family in that old world. My father died long ago, and my mother, the stranger whose blood floods my veins and soaks my canvases, over a decade ago. I think of my classmates, many of whom married and raised children and grandchildren in the same small town where we were all born. Leaving that place always felt to me like a lucky escape. A chance to break the cycle of suffering. I see my cousins, the ones who made it out, trying to do the same. Raising the next generation differently.

The chain of suffering is genetic. Parents pass on their traumas not only through their stories, their habits good and bad, but also through their genes. It takes the resilience of children to break that cycle. When I look at David and Mia, I know we've managed it. We've worked hard, but we've also been fortunate. When I see them happy, devoted to each other and their families, generous and loving, detached from material things, I know I have succeeded at the most important task in my life. Thanks to my sister, who helped me escape. Who believed in me, in my strength and my skill. At her funeral, I press my hands together and bow my head. In gratitude.

My life has come full circle. Each relationship, each kind of love, has its own weight. I've experienced them all. Passion, longing. Romance, adventure. Care, given and received. Empathy, compassion. Deep understanding. I've pursued different loves at different moments, and I've learned from every one. Each has been precious to me, though like different precious stones, their value changes over time.

Love is not about intuition. Feelings do not trump practicalities. Love is a skill, and it needs to be learned.

My time in Korea frees me. From my grief and anxiety, from the burden of unfinished business. As I prepare for the final phase of my journey, I am hopeful.

I wave my children off at the airport, back to their lives in the States. I've been invited to join a friend in India. To spend time in silence, among the trees and the birds. Another temple. My own pilgrimage. I am still my mother's daughter.

My interactions with my family and the country of my birth have generated creative ideas and inspiration, but retreating to a quiet place of reflection is essential as well. I need to spend a great deal of time at rest, focusing on my next idea. I've begun writing a book.

I've given away most of my clothes, gifted my favorite possessions to treasured friends and charities. My paintings adorn the walls of my children and my devoted collectors. I've left my apartment nearly empty. I don't know when I'll be back. I want to create more, consume less. Follow my passions deep down inside myself and see what more there is to discover in that deep, still well. I'm pursuing peace of mind. Every change is a mixed bag. But the only alterative is death. And I still have more living to do.

The challenges I've lived have taught me to make my own rules in life. The hardships I've faced have required my strength and given me freedom. But that freedom is limited. Every choice I've made has its advantages and disadvantages. My limitations have made me who I am. At this point in my life, I still have so much creative energy. I enjoy the surprise of the creative process, not as some divine gift, but as a skill I've cultivated over decades. Passion is not sufficient for great work. It is necessary, but there has to be more – risk and reflection, courage and love, sensitivity to the world and other people. Every day

I'm finding my balance between the unlimited possibilities of my imagination and the limitations of my reality.

The satisfaction and joy my creative work brings is more than worth the trade-off of the consequences of my choices, of choosing freedom over security. Because security is an illusion anyway. The freedom I have is the most valuable thing in my life. Giving unconditional love is the most meaningful. Receiving love is a corollary, but it is not the essential thing.

I remember my sister's words during one of our last conversations. I'd called to tell her about my efforts to downsize my life, to focus on what matters. To free myself of anything that depletes me. I was planning to visit her on my way to India. When she heard about my plans, about what I still hoped to achieve, she gave me one last piece of encouragement.

"Anything that does not fill you up is too small for you."

When I call Hélie from my hotel before the flight, I tell him I've rewritten our poem. "The Weight of Love." It has a new ending. All of our longing has brought us to a place of fullness, of healing. Of compassion, which is the real story of love. He is quiet for a moment after I read it to him.

"I never expected that at the end of my life, I would still be learning so much."

"Resilience," I tell him. The love song of my life. "There is always something new around the next corner."

"We are both students."

"And both teachers."

The past is written, and the future is unknowable. All we have is the present moment. That's our limitation, and our gift.

I am ready for the next adventure.

A Picture of Life

Life lives in
a chain of moments
linked in transition.

Relentlessly animated,
adaptive, marching on
with singular purpose.

Breathing through the present moment.
Keeping the past as a souvenir.
Waiting for an iridescent future.

As long as
emotion does not imprison us,
at least
we know what hope is:

The last thing to die.

Existence has no solution,
no amount of introspection.

Till journey's end
experiences
always remind us:

Life can only give
what it knows how.